"How Could Your Plans Involve Me?"

There was a tinge of panic in her voice, and a rush of protective feelings overwhelmed Quinn. He was tempted to reach out and straighten the broken antenna of the Grasshopper costume she had on for the festival, but it seemed too personal a gesture at the moment.

It was obvious that Kali was in no condition to listen to his announcement. He suspected the festival's special Grasshopper drink had been spiked.

"You were heading home, Kali. Why don't I give you a lift? We can talk over coffee. Come on, my Jeep is a short walk from here. And I think it's rather obvious you need someone to take care of you at the moment."

"Who elected you?"

"It was unanimous. I don't see any other candidates standing around, Kali. Believe me. You're about to find out I'm the best man for the job."

Dear Reader:

It's summertime, and I hope you've had a chance to relax and enjoy the season. Here to help you is a new man—Mr. August. Meet Joyce Thies's *Mountain Man*. He thinks he's conquered it all by facing Alaska, America's last frontier... but he hasn't met his mail-order bride yet!

Next month will bring a special man from Dixie Browning. Mr. September—Clement Cornelius Barto—is an unusual hero at best, but make no mistake, it's not just *Beginner's Luck* that makes him such a winner.

I hope you've been enjoying our "Year of the Man." From January to December, 1989 is a twelve-month extravaganza at Silhouette Desire. We're spotlighting one book each month with special cover treatment as a tribute to the Silhouette Desire hero—our *Man of the Month*!

Created by your favorite authors, these men are utterly irresistible. Don't let them get away!

Yours,

Isabel Swift
Senior Editor & Editorial Coordinator

NOREEN BROWNLIE
Race the Wind

Silhouette Desire

Published by Silhouette Books New York

America's Publisher of Contemporary Romance

SILHOUETTE BOOKS
300 East 42nd St., New York, N.Y. 10017

ISBN: 0-373-05513-7

First Silhouette Books printing August 1989

Printed in the U.S.A.

Books by Noreen Brownlie

Silhouette Desire

Savannah Lee #436
'Tis the Season #468
Race the Wind #513

NOREEN BROWNLIE

grew up in a large family on the Oregon coast, sur-rounded by Victorian houses, fishing boats and romantic sunsets. She met her husband while she was working inland as a television writer/producer, and the couple recently resettled in Seattle, where he continues to work in broadcasting and Noreen lives her dream of writing fiction full-time. There are always close family ties in her romances—a subject that is dear to her heart. Noreen has also written as Jamisan Whitney.

Dedicated with love and appreciation

to

Beverly Flint Fletcher

Thank you for calming the waters of self-doubt
and filling my sails with hope.

One

Quinn Sullivan frowned in disbelief as he reread the cheerful note tacked to the door of the old farmhouse.

Friends and neighbors,
Happy St. Uhro's Day! I'll be gone for a few hours to march in the parade. Join me if you're not busy. Be sure to wear green and purple. And may the wind be always at your back. Kali.

It had to be counterfeit. Either that or his new neighbor had gone through a drastic transformation during his five month absence. Kali Rainwater? Hadn't she done everything possible to make the real estate transaction more complicated than necessary, to make him thoroughly miserable last fall?

It was spooky.

People didn't change overnight.

As he walked back to his Jeep, Quinn turned and glanced toward the apple orchard where he'd first met Kali. She'd been dressed in faded jeans and a shapeless sweatshirt, but her raven-haired, dark-eyed beauty was branded in his memory. She was proud and beautiful and exuded inner strength, a plucky self-confidence that drew him to her.

In the depth of her eyes, in the clipped sentences, hurried movements, and references to boardsailors as "wind smurfs," he'd recognized something else. His father's philosophy of hard work.

Hard work had certainly not dulled Kali Rainwater, but it'd made her quick to judge. And it appeared she'd judged Quinn Sullivan, entrepreneur and boardsailor, to be unfit company. Her attitude was about to change. He'd see to that.

After starting the Jeep, Quinn steered it onto the highway leading to downtown Hood River.

His plan was simple. They were going to become good neighbors, and he was going to build a successful ice cream plant just as he had in Australia.

"It's high noon, folks! Time for all you grasshoppers to start hopping!"

Kali Rainwater watched as pickups started their engines. The largest of the three marching bands straightened their formation. Someone outfitted as St. Uhro, the patron saint famed for driving the grasshoppers out of the vineyards of Finland, raised his pitchfork high. Impaled on the tines was a four-foot papier-mâché grasshopper munching on purple grapes.

As laughter rippled through the crowd, Kali felt her spirits lift. This was her town. These were her people. Ninety percent of the participants were dressed as bugs, and for the first time, she'd chosen to join their ranks for the annual parade held on March 16th.

Kali glanced down at one of her hands. Like her arms and the tip of her nose, it was painted grasshopper-green for the event. She'd felt great about her costume when she left the house, but her confidence was fading. There were photographers...and her ever watchful brother, Morgan Rainwater, might be lurking.

"Heather, be honest—" she turned to her close friend and fellow orchardist "—do I look ridiculous?"

"We're dressed like grasshoppers. We're supposed to look ridiculous." Heather threw up her hands. "It's tradition! Lighten up. You've got to get in the spirit of this thing."

"What exactly is the spirit of this thing?"

"Tongue in cheek!" Heather gently tugged on one of Kali's antennae.

"Hien sirkka, hien sirkka, meme talta heeten!" the cry went up as the parade moved toward the crest of the hill that led down to the town proper.

"Hien h-hiena" Kali stumbled over the words the crowd was chanting, lacking the bilingual advantage of the many Finnish orchardists who populated the area. "What does it mean?" she asked the youthful blond grasshopper beside her.

"It's supposed to mean 'Grasshopper, grasshopper, go to hell,'" the teenage boy translated, his lopsided grin deepening.

As the fierce wind from the Columbia River Gorge gusted and caught her wings, Kali heard a communal gasp from the crowd. Human grasshoppers clutched at flailing antennae as wings rippled away from their bodies and created a magical illusion of floating gossamer. School-age grasshoppers, released early from classes to participate, laughed gleefully, their small wings aflutter as they raced to meet the next breeze.

Kali felt fully captured, caught in the festive web of mirth and merriment the event created. She almost lost a wing to a rambunctious preschooler twirling in blissful oblivion to the music of one of the three marching bands.

Heather caught the youngster before she spun out of control a second time. "It's good to see you smiling, Kali. Aren't you glad you took my advice and decided to spend a day away from the orchards and that blasted greenhouse?"

"You don't approve of my research?"

"Sure I do, I know how much the project means to you. I just don't like to see you working double time. If you're not in the orchards, you're in the greenhouse or your seedling fields with your strawberries. You need to find time—"

"Here it comes. The lecture on finding time for fun. Am I right?"

"Right." Heather was emphatic. "Like those boardsailors on the water. Look at 'em. They work hard, but they know how to play hard."

From their spectacular vantage point they could see the panorama of the Columbia River, the gorge and Washington State on the opposite shore. Despite the March chill, several brave boardsailors had ventured onto the water, challenging the wind and waves that had brought so many of their number to her tiny home town in Oregon.

Two more months and the multitude of boardsailors would include Quinn Sullivan. Did Heather expect her to forget that so easily?

"Work hard?" Kali questioned her friend's observation. "The only calluses those guys get are from hanging onto their booms while they duck jibe and—"

"Kali!" Heather turned so abruptly, her antennae bobbed up and down. "You're so, so—earthbound. Physical labor isn't the only hard work around. A lot of these people are doctors and lawyers, or they're in business for themselves. Some are just taking a hiatus from their career."

"We have careers, too. We're orchardists. When was the last time we had a nice long break?"

"I went to Hawaii last December. Don't you see? It's your strawberries, Kali. If you didn't have to worry about the breeding project, you'd be free to take time off every winter. Instead, you take it out on the boardsailors because they represent the freedom you don't have. Isn't that true?"

It was the very truth Kali wasn't willing to face. "You know, I think it's time to change the subject. We're marching in a parade." Kali smiled and held out her arm for an impromptu do-si-do with Heather.

"I've got to stay in the spirit of this thing, remember?"

Quickly but with some difficulty, she refocused her attention on the parade. *"Hien sirkka! Hien sirkka!"* she joined in the chant.

As they neared Hood River's downtown area, the sidewalks were lined with spectators. The St. Uhro Day queen and her royal court threw mint candies wrapped in green foil to the cheering crowd.

When the parade stopped to let the lead band play a rousing version of the Finnish national anthem, the younger participants began hopping in place. Laughing, Kali reached out to help another costumed child steady himself.

For some inexplicable reason, her gaze was suddenly drawn to the colorful awning over one of the numerous shops selling gear for boardsailors. And lower, to the arresting sight of a tall, dark-haired man in jungle attire who tipped his bush hat and smiled at her. Quinn Sullivan had returned to Hood River—two months early. She felt numb from disbelief. It was too soon. She'd been working on changing her attitude, but Dear God, she needed the extra time.

"Kali, isn't that Quinn What's-his-name—the guy who bought your land?" Heather used the discretion of a bull moose as she shouted her query.

Ignoring Heather and the distracting male mirage, Kali struggled to focus on the child jumping up and down in front of her.

"I'm a boardsailor!" the boy shouted. "Let's pretend I'm a boardsailor! Here comes a wave!"

The parade moved on, but Kali felt as though she were drenched with conflicting emotions, struggling to surface from the impact of the not-so-imaginary wave, the shock of seeing Quinn.

The Kali he knew wouldn't be in this parade. She wouldn't even be in the crowd of cheering, raucous spectators. Yet, for some odd reason, Quinn couldn't stop feeling she was here, that the note on her door had been genuine.

"...the parade is actually an import from a town in Minnesota. Local fella started doing it here about ten years ago I guess. People took to dressin' as insects only recently, but it's catchin' on fast...."

The man next to him had been giving his fellow spectators a brief history of the event, but Quinn could only listen with half an ear. At first he'd pushed the brim of his hat back in disbelief when the city's main street was suddenly filled with chanting human grasshoppers—on foot, high atop farm machinery, in pickups, on horseback, in marching formation and tiny bugs in arms. The quiet picturesque town he'd entered that morning had turned into a chaotic carnival of green and purple.

And then he saw her. Kali Rainwater. Laughing, her smile radiant, her costume outrageous but beguiling. The green T-shirt, jogging shorts and tights outlined her tall slender body, but it was her smile he focused on. When the parade participants began jumping in place, she helped the youngster in front of her, offering words of encouragement as she lifted him up to exaggerate each bounce.

Quinn was enthralled by this playful side of Kali. As he edged through the throng of spectators for a closer look, her gaze shifted. Their eyes met for a brief moment, and then she turned away, absorbed with the jumping child.

There had been a flicker of recognition in her eyes just before he tipped his hat. Was it his imagination, or was Kali simply refusing to acknowledge his presence?

He turned to the historian at his elbow. "Excuse me. Where does the parade disband?"

"Hold still, honey." Using his wife's back, the man traced the path with his finger. "It's right here, near the shoulder blade."

"Thanks." Quinn shook the man's hand.

"By the way, they serve grasshoppers at the end of the parade. Course, not everyone cares for the taste."

"I've been living in Australia for half a dozen years," Quinn explained. "I've had everything from Vegemite to kangaroo. How do they cook 'em? Stir-fry, boil—"

The older man looked bewildered.

"What is it?" Quinn frowned. He was anxious to find Kali.

"You'll see, young man. Just follow my directions and *bon appétit.*"

As she stood at the next street corner, listening to the band, Kali's spirits sagged momentarily. Much as she tried to fight her true feelings, she couldn't deny them. Quinn was a reminder of her failed promises to her father and brother.

Just when her credit had been exhausted and her dream of marketing a new variety of strawberry threatened, Quinn stopped by her orchards to ask about the view property. It wasn't for sale, of course. Kali was saving the acreage for the dream house she'd planned since childhood. One of the best views for miles around.

But Quinn's offer promised a rescue for her strained finances, hope for her strawberry.

Her brother, Morgan, was adamantly against the sale. He reminded Kali of the promise she'd made their father before his death two years ago. She'd preserve the land—all of it.

But she'd had few choices. In a matter of weeks, she'd signed the Rainwater name to the papers. Her most prized piece of land, the only acreage that wasn't zoned for farm use, now belonged to Quinn. Her part-Chinook grandfather had laid the foundation for a new family home in the forties. The weathered bricks had stood as a monument to perseverance for her. The bricks were gone now. Construction had begun on the Sullivan house.

With the sale, she gave up yet another dream. She had few dreams in her repertoire to give up, but they were succumbing to the cost of financing her horticultural experiments.

Who had said a goal was a dream with a deadline? A famed philosopher, or someone who worked the soil and understood the challenges she faced?

The season lasted May through October for board-sailors in the gorge. A small number chose to stay year round, but Quinn Sullivan had made it clear he'd be a half-a-year resident. What worried her most was the fact that he was also becoming a full-time resident of her thoughts.

Kali smiled to herself. She wasn't giving up or giving in to defeat. At moments like this, it was best to simply reaffirm the promise she'd made to herself last winter.

In time, her breeding project would be successful. With the profits, Kali promised anew, she'd buy her view property—and everything on it—back from Quinn Sullivan.

The parade was over. Quinn moved along the edge of the swarm of spectators until he came to the area where bands, bugs and orchard buggies dispersed.

An informal beer garden was set up in the clearing beyond. Couples danced to accordion music. Quinn studied the female grasshoppers searching for a glimpse of black hair and dancing brown eyes. Finding Kali in this sea of green was going to be near impossible.

As he moved back through the crowd, Quinn stopped and talked to a number of local people he'd met the year before. Merchants, boardsailors who'd settled in the area, and the landlord who'd rented an apartment to him last summer. Did anyone escape grasshopper fever in this town? The familiar faces gave him a sense of belonging.

The pieces were falling in place with clockwork precision. He'd been more than pleased with the progress on the warehouse renovation project. Starting a successful American ice cream plant had been his primary goal for two years. Taking time out for board-sailing and exploring the scenic Hood River Valley was a priority that had been moved down a notch or two on his list. It was his home, little more than cement and a blueprint at this point, that had taken on an unexpected importance in his mind. He wanted to feel connected to this community.

Turning, Quinn looked up the hill to the promise of rolling orchard land beyond the crest. He'd viewed the property this morning. The rubble had been cleared. The foundation for his new home had been poured. Plans called for an August completion date.

The motor home that would be his combined living quarters and office for the next six months was due to arrive tomorrow. It was important that Kali Rainwater know he planned to become her next-door neighbor much sooner than expected. Damn. It was essential he talk to Kali now.

"I never liked crème de menthe, and I'm not about to learn because of some saint. Take this—please." Inside the beer garden, an elderly great-aunt placed another cold frosty grasshopper in Kali's palm. "It's spiked a bit, so go easy."

She laughed and nodded her thanks, then moved on through the crowd in search of friends and neighbors.

After mingling for an hour, Kali came to a realization. Every orchardist in the valley was heading into the same busy schedule, yet they talked about their personal lives. They still had interests and social lives outside of their farms. How long had it been since she'd slipped away to see a movie, or traveled to Portland or the Oregon coast just for the fun of it?

Heather was right. She was too "earthbound."

Time after time, Kali listened to her peers describe their winter getaways, or compare skiing holidays on nearby Mount Hood. She hadn't skied for years. When she wasn't tied down with her orchard work, it was her research. Or was it? Her brother Morgan and nephew Travis lived on the adjoining land. Travis had frequently volunteered to help her with with the breeding project's operation and record keeping. Why had she been so eager to turn the teenager down?

There was no beer in the beer garden, only tall frosty grasshoppers, the traditional St. Uhro Day drink. She sipped the minty drink in her hand and attempted to look somewhat dignified. She rarely drank, but the need to discard the doldrums of the past winter, to celebrate the season of rebirth welled within her. This was her private festival.

The coming spring heralded new hope. The land had slipped from her fingers. What was done was done. It was a reality she had to confront, but she needed more time. So what if Quinn Sullivan had arrived two months early?

The man was an enigma. Many of the boardsailors were young professionals who could afford the travel and equipment expenses. Others were "wind bums." Kali felt a need to categorize her neighbor to be. During their brief meetings about the sale, Quinn had been open about his love for boardsailing on the gorge. He'd made a few vague references to his being in business for himself.

Entrepreneur. It could mean anything in this rapidly expanding town. But it was obvious Quinn had the resources to pay a high price for her land and to finance construction of a house.

Was he a spoiled rich boy who would buckle under the strain of an honest day's labor? The man was used to the luxury of hiring others to do his work. Before he left to "follow the wind" to Australia, Quinn handed the business of building the house over to a local contractor. She felt a twinge of envy.

For the past few weeks, while the weather warmed, she'd walked through her orchards contemplating the man whose life was a stark contrast to her own. But the memory of Quinn's warm gaze, impressive physique and easy smile had played on her mind since his departure. How often had she raised her nose from the grindstone to contemplate the return of Quinn Sullivan?

"Here, take my drink. Can't stand the taste of the things. Too sweet." A middle-aged female cousin took Kali's glass and offered her a fresh grasshopper. "It's good to see you smiling and looking so happy. I swear your whole life revolves around that farm. You turned out just like your late father, you know."

"How's that?" Kali ventured, her inhibitions lifting. She knew full well what the answer would be. Her mother's side of the family made a game of comparing and contrasting offspring and siblings.

"You're working yourself into an early grave. Now mind your wings, honey."

"My wings?"

"You're moving to the music, fluttering around like a bee. Maybe you should slow down on those drinks, sweetie."

Kali attempted to take a mental inventory, but the count was fuzzy. "The relatives keep passing their unwanted drinks off on me."

"Well, that explains the flutter. You call me when you decide to go home. I'll give you a lift."

"Fine. I feel fine," Kali tried to reassure the feisty gray-haired woman. "But I'd appreciate the lift just the same. I caught a ride to the parade in a neighbor's truck."

"Okay, you just holler, honey. You know me. I'll be dancing."

Kali laughed as her cousin grabbed the hand of a male bystander and pulled him into the circle of dancers. She would have followed the older woman, but Kali's path was blocked by a male chest draped in a forest green shirt and faded khaki jacket. Holding tight to her remaining antenna, she tilted her head upward and recognized the weathered bush hat before she was able to focus fully on the tanned angular features of Quinn Sullivan.

This was not the neutral encounter she'd pictured in her mind. She'd lost an antenna, torn a wing and felt high enough to fly.

"It's good to see you, Kali." He reached up to brush the brim of his hat with his fingertips.

"Well, look what the wind blew in." She spoke the first words that came to mind and instantly regretted them.

Two

Look what the wind blew in?

Her subtle sarcasm didn't escape him. Quinn lowered his hand slowly and let it settle on his hip. Last fall Kali seldom offered a smile, or anything beyond a perfunctory comment. She'd struck him as a woman too caught up in her work to enjoy the scenic splendor or romantic prospects abounding in the Columbia River Gorge. Had he honestly expected her to change?

It was evident she hadn't altered her feelings about him.

She was staring at him and managing to look quite serious and quite beautiful despite the costume. He broadened his smile, hoping to ease the tension of the moment.

Kali fought through a web of panic. She wasn't ready to confront a flesh and blood Quinn Sullivan. She'd spent a winter contemplating the man who'd changed her life. Now he was back, threatening to steal the magic from her springtime—or to add to it.

Was that her real fear? The fear of being attracted to Quinn?

His faded jungle fatigues accentuated his impressive physique, adding to his rugged appeal. The rise in his imperfect nose was easy to overlook unless one chose to ponder how he'd broken it. Was it any easier to stare intently at the riveting blue of Quinn's eyes? Kali made no effort to put a name to their color. It was best described by emotion. Untamed, mirthful, impetuous, fearless. With just a hint of sadness.

"The name is Quinn in case you've forgotten."

"I hadn't forgotten your name, Mr. Sullivan." She extended her hand with hesitation. Kali was tempted to withdraw, but held her hand out, waiting. She knew the warmth of his fingers entwining with hers would make the reality of his presence more unbearable. "I'm just surprised to see you in March. The dormant pears have barely started to bud."

While she spoke, he slipped his hand in hers. His touch held an uncommon warmth, and he had the strong sinewy fingers of a boardsailor.

"Your body looks great," he said without missing a beat. Suddenly she wished she'd put the green makeup on her face. It would have hidden the crimson blush. "I mean your costume, Kali," he added quickly. "Head, thorax and abdomen, isn't it?"

Quinn released her hand but she felt the burning brand of his gaze.

It was important for her to be on an even footing with people. When and why had Quinn gained the advantage? In less than a minute, with an economy of words, using body heat, humor and a smile, the man had managed to unnerve her.

"What are you doing here?" she asked in a tone intended to intimidate. Instead her voice wavered and seemed thick with emotion.

"I figured the prettiest female grasshopper in town would be dancing in the beer garden."

This wasn't working. She'd made Quinn the catch-all villain in her winter musings. The only thing villainous about him now was his ability to evade her questions and the sense of danger she felt in his presence.

Where were inhibitions when you needed them? Kali looked down at the drink in her hand. Leaving the orchards and joining a public spectacle had been her first mistake. Losing track of the vodka-laced grasshoppers had been her second. She set her half-empty glass on a passing tray.

Quinn watched the play of emotion on Kali's features. She appeared to be struggling with an inner thought. Perhaps the invisible and undefined fences that stood between them were being torn down. He'd welcomed the handshake. How could he forget the afternoon last fall when Kali had refused his offer of a handshake at the completion of the sale?

He didn't want to give her time to think about the past. It was his habit to move forward in all things. No regrets. No looking back. Make way for the new.

"Come on. They're playing our song." He grabbed Kali's hand and moved toward the ever-growing circle of dancers. "Please excuse the informal invitation to dance—" he whirled her into his arms "—but I've been sitting on a plane and in a rental car for what seems like days. I need to move around."

"Our song?" Kali was still surprised by Quinn's sudden desire to dance. "All these songs sound alike to me."

"Trust me. This one's special." He laughed when she widened her eyes.

How long had it been since she'd danced? Two years? Three? The song became special because the experience was special. Her private celebration of the new spring had blossomed to include Quinn Sullivan. Her movements became livelier, her laughter less subdued.

"I saw you in the parade earlier," he spoke in a near shout over the accordion music. "I envy the way you're so involved with the community."

"Actually I've been too busy to get involved in most events," she corrected. "This is my first encounter with the mysterious St. Uhro."

"My compliments. You looked like a veteran out there. Must run in the blood. The people here know how to have a good time."

Kali smiled weakly. If only Quinn knew the truth of it. She'd forced herself to buy the material to make the costume and begrudged the time devoted to the project. There was a point when she believed a love of fun ran in her Rainwater veins. But that period had passed. For her, pleasure had become a distraction rather than a pastime.

Kali glanced around at her fellow townspeople. The beer garden looked like a scene out of a bizarre mating ritual. More than fifty human grasshoppers danced, rubbing wings and playing havoc with their delicate exoskeletons. The costumes weren't built for speed, crowds or a polka rhythm.

One lively tune followed another in rapid succession. There was little time to analyze her actions or to question the wisdom of a productive afternoon spent in the arms of a near stranger. She was lost in sensation, giddy from the vodka, and drunk on the feelings Quinn evoked in her.

Quinn tightened his hold on her waist and drew her against his chest when the music slowed. "It's good to see you enjoying yourself, Kali."

Why would he notice such a thing? she wondered with a sudden sense of unease. As she moved in a slow circle, she focused her gaze on Quinn's face in an effort to read his thoughts. Why had he returned two months early? Where would he stay, and how would he occupy his time? Quinn's eyes were shadowed by the brim of his bush hat, thwarting her efforts to find clues to the answers.

"I've thought about you often since I left Hood River."

A door opened within her when he spoke. She yearned to tell him the same thing, to describe the lonely hours she'd spent staring into the firelight and contemplating his return. He was here now, and so real and warm and charming.

"If you've thought of me, Kali, I hope your thoughts have been kind."

"Confused." Had he heard her response? "I've had a lot to think about, Quinn, and unlike Australia, we were going through winter here. Snow, cold winds, rain. Not the kind of weather a boardsailer would enjoy."

"I may be a California native, Kali, but I spent five years at Harvard. I remember those winters fondly."

"Harvard?"

"Does that surprise you?"

She didn't answer. Quinn was full of surprises. She couldn't continue dancing like this and chance telling him the truth. Their lives were going to be hopelessly entangled if she didn't pull away from the web Quinn was weaving around her. Word games and intimate glances. Kali slowed her dancing, then stopped. She'd been a fool to get caught up in his easy rapport.

"Thank you for inviting me to dance, but I have to leave now." To hide her embarrassment and frustration, she used a polite smile and tea party tone to excuse herself. It was a combination she hadn't conjured up since sixth grade. "I'm afraid I have work waiting for me at the farm."

After turning to leave, she immediately felt one of her wings connect with his body, heard the soft escape of his breath and the curse that followed.

Kali kept moving and was two feet from the beer garden exit when her costume snagged. She looked over her shoulder. Quinn was standing behind her, exerting a firm grip on a gossamer wing.

She tugged back. "Excuse me."

"Kali—"

Quinn moved closer. Or pulled her toward him. She was too dizzy and disoriented to distinguish the difference.

"Kali, I really need to talk to you. It's about the plans I'm making for this spring. They involve you in a roundabout way."

"How could your plans involve me?"

There was a tinge of panic in her voice, a vulnerability that touched him. A rush of protective feelings overwhelmed Quinn. He still had no idea how she felt about him. He was tempted to reach out and straighten the broken antenna, but it seemed too personal a gesture at the moment.

It was obvious Kali was in no condition to listen to his announcement. They'd stopped dancing, but her giddiness remained, her eyes were slightly unfocused, unnaturally bright. He suspected the grasshopper drink. He'd taken one sip, relieved to know the name referred to a cocktail and not an hors d'oeuvre sporting insect legs.

"You were heading home, Kali. Why don't I give you a lift in my Jeep? We can talk over coffee."

"Thank you, but I have a ride with my cousin—the woman dancing with St. Uhro."

"There are three people dressed as the good saint."

"Well, she's wearing a purple banner over her, uh, thorax."

"Uh-huh, the one with the mandibles. Interesting touch," Quinn noted aloud. "But even from here, I can see she's tipsier than you are. Come on, my Jeep is a short walk from here." He put a hand on Kali's shoulder. "That red flush is getting deeper by the minute."

"I'm just a little overheated from the costume."

"Overheated from a T-shirt and shorts?"

"Do you always make such ridiculous assumptions?"

"I don't make assumptions. I never assume anything unless I'm right. And I think it's rather obvious you need someone to take care of you at the moment."

"Who elected you?"

"It was unanimous. I don't see any other candidates standing around, Kali. Believe me. You're about to find out I'm the best man for the job."

"Go ahead. I'll make the coffee while you change."

Kali stood in the kitchen doorway, staring in wonder at the tall man who was opening her cupboards and asserting himself in her home. "The filters are—"

"I'll find them," he assured her. "Are you hungry?"

"Hmmm. A bit." She nodded. It was four o'clock and she hadn't eaten since fixing a small supper the night before.

"Then I'll cook something that isn't green or minty, all right?"

Kali gave him a faint smile before turning to sidle down the hall. The wings and hind legs that prevented easy movement were soon dispensed with.

She could hear noises coming from the kitchen. Hadn't she had her fill of pushy men? Her father seemed to have perfected the trait before passing it on to her brother. Quinn was demonstrating remarkable skill at being mulish . . . and mysterious.

A hot shower washed away all evidence of green paint. She put on her uniform of faded blue jeans and T-shirt and laced up the cleanest pair of sneakers she could find. After wiping steam off the antiquated bathroom mirror, she ran a comb through her damp hair and added a touch of makeup to her face.

She'd considered herself rather attractive in college. Her silky dark hair, large eyes, and high cheekbones had prompted questions about the country of her origin. The happy days spent at Oregon State University seemed long ago. Duty had called her home. Guilt had kept her there. The strain of long hours and hard work had to show. When was the last time she considered herself beautiful? Self-doubt nagged at Kali. What chance did she have to compete against the globe-trotting female boardsailors for Quinn's attention?

"Listen to yourself!" She hissed at her reflection, leaning closer to the mirror. "He's here to talk business not pleasure, and you're wasting time in the bathroom building sand-castle dreams. Get your butt out to the kitchen and sober up—pronto."

For a moment, Kali's heart twisted with an indefinable pain. "Go easy. Be kind to yourself." She rested a fingertip against the mirror and sighed. What was so wrong with hoping for happiness, wanting the impossible, taking chances?

When she reached the small farmhouse kitchen, Quinn had sandwiches wrapped, fruit laid out on the table, and he was filling a thermos with fresh aromatic coffee.

"How about a picnic?" he asked. "We can walk to my property."

"Your property?"

"What do you want me to call the land I bought from you?"

Straightening her shoulders, she walked to the cupboard and took two insulated mugs from the shelf.

"The picnic sounds great. If we're lucky, we'll catch one of those beautiful sunsets I never have time to appreciate." The words sounded sharper than she'd intended. Quickly she busied herself with packing the thermos, food and mugs into a small backpack, then threw in a small packet of cat snacks. "Don't worry. I'm packing those for Blossom."

"Your cat?"

"Cat, champion mouser and trusted companion. She'll come bounding after us by the time we get to my—excuse me—your property." The pronoun that represented so much loss to her came easier than she expected. Perhaps the healing had begun.

Kali smiled to herself as she watched Quinn shoulder the pack. The giddy sensations from the grasshoppers were dissipating. There was no longer any excuse for the warm capricious feeling she was experiencing.

* * *

"This will be the living room." Quinn moved from one section of the spacious foundation to another, gesturing as he described the design of each room. Kali followed, nodding her head, smiling solemnly and closing her eyes each time she brought the mug of coffee to her lips.

It was obvious to Quinn his tour of imagined rooms was causing her pain. Her expression had been one of openness and wonder during their picnic on the grass further up the ridge. As they dined on sandwiches and fruit, Kali had talked about the parade and answered his questions about events that had occurred in Hood River over the winter months. The easy banter was gone now.

"So both the back and front of your house will be glass?"

"Almost," he answered. "With these gorge winds I had to have plenty of support, but there'll be windows fore and aft. I made sure your view of the ridge won't be destroyed, Kali."

"I'll be able to see the entire panorama—as long as you keep your drapes open, right?" Her words were spoken in a teasing tone, but her smile was less then convincing.

"Right. And there won't be any drapes."

"Tinted windows?"

"No. I like openness. Honesty. I have nothing to hide."

"But privacy...."

"I believe privacy is a state of mind, Kali. I like things natural. I want to feel the elements, see the sky, hear the full impact of the wind, watch the whitecaps on the water.''

Her expression was wistful. Perhaps she'd dreamed of building a home here, Quinn pondered. Maybe she understood why he'd chosen this piece of heaven. He poured coffee into his empty mug and sat down on the concrete block foundation. "Do you want to tell me about this property, why it means so much to you?"

Kali put down her cup, bent to pick up Blossom, then settled a short distance from Quinn on the ledge of concrete. The first faint ribbons of red-orange streaked down the Columbia River, illuminating her profiled features and the cat's white fur with a warm glow. She turned to face him, her expression wistful, distant.

"This was my grandfather's favorite thinking spot. He and Grandma Rainwater lived in the farmhouse I own now. Back in the forties they started to build a new home on the ridge, but they never finished more than the foundation." Kali rubbed the area under Blossom's chin with an absent gesture then paused. "Grampa came up here every spring and arranged and rearranged the piles of bricks. I think he needed to keep his finger on the dream."

"What happened to the dream?"

"He passed it on to my father who passed it on to me, and then I sold it to you, Quinn."

Her words were abrupt, stark, unadorned. Quinn felt a sharp twisting pain between his ribs. Her soft hushed voice, free of any accusations, doubled the impact of the simple statement.

The cat stepped out of Kali's lap onto the ledge, then jumped down to the cement and began investigating the foundation. Quinn moved closer.

"What are you thinking?" he asked.

Kali felt a brick in some inner wall give. She studied his face intently. With his hat off, Quinn looked younger. In the glow of sunset, his tanned angular features were more clearly defined. The strong jaw and easy smile reminded her that this man was California born and bred. Ocean beaches, sun-kissed bodies, open feelings. He was asking her how she felt, and she was overwhelmed by a desire to share her thoughts.

"Every time I take the short walk to this ridge I feel like I'm walking back in time. I'm a child again. Dancing in the wind. No limits to the imagination, no pressures, no looming realities."

He didn't speak. His warm gaze prompted her to continue.

"This was my stage, Quinn, this short stretch of land. I can see why my grandfather treasured it. For years I used to sneak away from my chores to playact here. I alternated between Indian princess and frontier woman, cowgirl and Johnny Appleseed. I don't know how it slipped from my hands as quickly as it did."

"If I had known, Kali..." Quinn started.

"No. Don't apologize." Kali swallowed hard and closed her eyes. The day would come. She'd buy his land and the two-story house and Lord knows what.

The echo of sadness in her voice touched him. Where was the smiling, laughing woman he'd danced with this afternoon? Quinn reached out. His fingertips pressed gently along the edge of her jaw until she was turned to face him fully. She opened her eyes slowly.

The lashes were starred with moisture, but the emotion in her luminous brown eyes was unfathomable. What had he expected to find in their depths? Self-pity or sorrow? She blinked, and there was a flickering sheen of fierce pride and conviction. Only her half-parted mouth revealed the vulnerability he'd heard so clearly in her voice.

Quinn was about to become a part of her life. He wanted to know how Kali felt about him. More importantly, he wanted to share his strength without the encumbrance of words.

Quinn smoothed windblown strands of hair back from her cheek with his fingertips and lifted the fleece-lined collar of her jacket. Her skin was flushed with the hues of sunset, or was that the afterglow of the festive St. Uhro Day grasshoppers?

"Still a bit light-headed, Ms. Rainwater?" he asked, moving his thumb to the edge of her mouth.

"No. I never was." Her smile was faint, but he felt the movement against the pad of his thumb. "I'm too down-to-earth for that, Mr. Sullivan."

He brushed his thumb against the tantalizing fullness of her lower lip. Her mouth closed and opened, and he heard the gentle intake of her breath.

"Are you too down-to-earth—" leaning closer, he brought his mouth down to her half-parted lips until their breaths mingled "—for this, Kali?" Quinn heard her moan softly before she narrowed the space and made the kiss complete.

Kali closed her eyes against the sensations. Quinn's arms moved around her, and his fingers caught in her hair as the kiss intensified. The striated orange-gold colors of the fiery sunset swirled through her random thoughts like a second embrace. His hands smelled faintly of the oranges he'd peeled for their dinner.

Even the brisk gorge wind seemed warm against her cheek as she let herself float in sensations long forgotten. Then just as quickly as she'd lost herself, she pulled back. "No, Quinn. I'm sorry."

"Kali, what's wrong?" His hand touched her elbow.

She stood up and began gathering their things into the backpack. "Where are you spending the night?" she asked more abruptly than intended.

Quinn looked startled. He took a deep breath. "I planned to pitch my tent here, right here inside the foundation."

"With this wind?"

"Up until a few seconds ago, I wasn't aware of the chill." There was a hint of irritation in his voice. He picked up his hat and placed it slowly on his head, pulling the brim down slightly on his forehead.

She shrugged the comment off, more upset with herself than she was with him. The man had just arrived in town. Where was her hospitality? "You might as well put the tent in my shed. You can use my shower in the morning and have some breakfast."

"Thank you," he murmured, taking the backpack from her and slinging it over his shoulder.

They began walking toward the farmhouse. "Quinn, you said something earlier about discussing your plans for the spring. Something about these plans involving me.''

''They do. I'm having a motor home delivered to this site tomorrow. I'll be living in it until the house is finished, using it as an office and residence. It shouldn't be in your way, but I wanted you to know I'll be your neighbor much sooner than expected.''

Kali watched the last vestiges of scarlet leave the sky as Quinn spoke. The sun was down, but this day continued to unfurl surprises for her. Hearing the hammers and saws would be difficult enough without the presence of this wealthy, free-spirited man.

''I'm heading into one of my busiest seasons,'' she said flatly. ''So we better get a few things straight from the beginning. I can't afford to hire as much help as I did last year. I'll be too busy to even open the door and let you borrow so much as a cup of sugar.''

''I understand. I believe I heard another variation of this speech before. Last September. You didn't have time to smile or make small talk—or shake hands.''

''It was during harvest. Where I come from, Quinn, work is a priority.''

''So, I'm still the dreaded wind smurf.''

They'd reached the gravel path that led to her porch. Kali crunched ahead of him in silence, anxious to avoid a confrontation. Her hand was on the ornate wooden rail.

''Everywhere I go, there's talk about the warmth and friendliness of the people of this town. I'm curious. Why are you so different, Kali?''

The impact of his words hit her fully. ''If you keep walking, Mr. Sullivan, you'll find the shed.''

"I'd rather keep talking. But for some reason it bothers you that I asked, doesn't it?"

Her hand was on the doorknob. "If you want to talk about how cold and unfriendly you find me, I'm not interested."

"Actually, I'd like to talk about your work schedule." He sat back against the porch rail. "You must have a few days here and there you can set aside for someone like me."

"Exactly what are you, Quinn?" she asked as she opened the front door.

"A man who likes a challenge. I'd like to see you take more time for the beautiful things in life, Kali. Starting soon." With that comment, he smiled and tipped his hat. Placing one hand on the railing, Quinn vaulted to the gravel path below and disappeared into the twilight.

From her upstairs window, Kali could see the diffused glow of Quinn's lantern. He'd pitched his tent just outside her shed. The man was daring, defiant and stubborn. All the more reason to keep her distance.

The second blur of light wasn't a lantern. Recognizing Blossom's snow-white fur, she smiled to herself. Only a heartless person would deny anyone the company of a cat—but she felt a special need for her longtime companion tonight.

She got into bed slowly, bracing herself. The sheets were cool against her bare legs. She'd never conceded to the comfort of flannel, not even in winter. She'd worn too many flannel shirts in her lifetime and would probably die in one. Leave flannel for the fields. When it came to nightwear, she ordered Victorian lace and cotton blends from mail-order catalogs. Her lingerie was a well-kept secret. Too well-kept. Not since college had any man been presented with the opportunity to explore the sexy underthings that lay against her skin.

She turned over and glanced toward the window. Though she couldn't hear or see Quinn, she was fully cognizant of his presence. How could she dismiss the memory of their brief kiss?

Perhaps it was too soon to be sure, but Quinn seemed to be everything she didn't want in a man. If she let him into her life, he'd become a constant distraction. She didn't have time to dwell on a boardsailor who said what he felt without thinking of the consequences.

She'd show him. By the end of the summer, Quinn would be the foolish grasshopper, and she'd be the prudent ant. And what would that prove? Kali pulled the coverlet over her shoulder. Life wasn't a fable. It was real. As real as the loneliness that had enveloped her nightly for six years.

Three

———

"Thanks for the use of the shower. I feel human again." Quinn leaned against the doorjamb, pushing his damp hair back with his fingers while he observed the scene in the kitchen.

Kali cracked an egg into a bowl on the stove before looking up. She'd set the table while he showered. Early morning sunlight streamed through the kitchen windows, highlighting the ethereal scene in the cheerful yellow kitchen. Red strawberries, blue plates, a glowing white tablecloth. Kali continued staring at him. Her red T-shirt was tucked into her jeans, her hair pulled back in a loose braid that hung over her shoulder.

"I hope pancakes are all right." Her voice was level, devoid of emotion. Yet the warmth in her gaze was evident.

"Sounds great, but I don't want to put you through any trouble." Picking up a mug from the table, Quinn filled it with fresh coffee, and freshened the cup at Kali's elbow. She'd invited him to breakfast and offered the use of her shower last night, but this morning Quinn felt he was straining her hospitality.

"What do you grow in the big greenhouse?"

She poured batter onto the griddle in four symmetrical circles. "I use it for my research."

"What kind of research?"

"I'm working on a new variety of strawberry. Have been for almost six years."

"So you have a background in horticulture?"

She smiled slowly, as if to herself. There was a rush of excitement in her voice as she described her college studies.

"...and soon after I was admitted to an advance program toward my doctorate, Dad had his stroke. I came home to help out—" she paused before flipping the last pancake over "—and I never went back to school. The greenhouse and seedling fields are used for my breeding project. I've been forced to choose between buying new equipment for the orchards and investing the money in my research."

"And what comes first, Kali?" Quinn leaned back against the counter and took a sip of coffee.

"The family's land, of course, the orchards. My father died from a second stroke, Quinn. I can't walk through the fields without thinking of Dad pruning, spraying, working with the crews, harvesting, and carrying smudge pots." She flipped the pancakes onto a platter and began pouring more batter onto the griddle. "My credit ran out last year. No more loans on something as experimental as my berries. So I sold the land to cover future expenses."

That explained it. Quinn lowered his cup slowly. She was duty bound to this land through her love for her father and grandfather. She had every right to feel frustrated, to resent him. He would have to take this slowly. The desire to protect her, to share his strength, was overwhelming. But he couldn't ignore the pride in the thrust of her chin.

"I know Oregonians are famed for their rugged individualism, Kali. Sometimes to a fault. Do you get much help with the orchard work?"

"I can't handle the cost of hiring a foreman anymore but I have a good crew. They're like family to me now."

"You mentioned a brother last night."

"Morgan. When Dad died, the property was split, and Morgan got the land closest to the acreage he inherited from my maternal grandparents. So he and his son Travis live on the property adjoining mine. I got the land closest to the house and to the properties I inherited from my paternal grandparents. Confused yet?"

"Where's your mother?"

"She sold the house in town after Dad died and lives in Portland with her sister. She's not overly enthusiastic about life on the farm anymore. She's still bitter about Dad's death. But she keeps in touch with Morgan and me and visits as often as she can."

"It must be nice to have close family ties."

"Sometimes. My brother's quite a bit older than I am, and I'll warn you, he's more than a little protective."

Quinn admired this woman. Kali had explained the situation without a trace of self-pity in her tone. In fact, she seemed to grow stronger, stand straighter as she spoke.

As she brought the platter of pancakes to the table, there was the sound of tires on gravel. She was transformed again as she moved toward the window. Her gestures were suddenly halting, less natural. He was touched by the sudden display of vulnerability.

"I was afraid of this. It's Morgan. And he's brought my nephew Travis."

"And you're worried that he'll think I spent the night with you, aren't you?"

"It's a conclusion anyone might reach. Why don't you sit down while I get the door."

Quinn couldn't make out all of the conversation in the living room but he heard his name and the words "motor home" and "tent."

Morgan Rainwater entered the kitchen moments later and studied Quinn in silence before he poured himself a cup of coffee. Travis was more open about his interest. Both were above average height, with rugged good looks. The dark hair and eyes, and tanned even features seemed to run in the family. While Morgan exuded a quiet strength, his son moved with restless energy.

After Kali quickly introduced them, the men shook hands.

"I saw the Jeep out front and thought I better check on things," Morgan explained. "Kali says you're the boardhead who bought our land."

"It was my land, Morgan," Kali hastened to correct. "Look, we were just about to sit down. I'll make up more pancakes and you can join us."

For the next twenty minutes, fifteen-year-old Travis barraged Quinn with questions about boardsailing while Morgan made pointed remarks about the changing face of their small city. Travis's adulation of Quinn was soon evident and only added to the tension.

Kali looked up to find Quinn's less-than-subtle gaze aimed in her direction. She felt a sudden stirring, a desire to reach out and tell Quinn she found him warm and attractive, that she welcomed his presence as a neighbor and looked forward to developing a friendship.

"Come on, Travis, we should be going," Morgan interrupted her reverie. "Looks like your Aunt Kali took a day of vacation yesterday and she'll need to catch up on her work."

There had been no need for Morgan to speak. Kali had seen the accusing look in her brother's eyes long before. She'd always been able to read his moods, or had she just assumed he was always disapproving?

She was certain of one thing. Morgan was still furious that she had sold prime acreage to a boardsailor. After their father's estate was settled, Morgan had been filled with resentment, accusing Kali of getting the best orchards, expressing concern that she'd marry and work the land with a man who didn't share her respect for it. Morgan had wanted the land for his son Travis, a legacy to pass on to the next generation of Rainwaters.

"So when are you takin' your board out?"

While Travis asked one more question of Quinn, Kali began clearing dishes. Arrogant or not, Morgan was right. She did have chores to catch up on, as well as other responsibilities. How could she expect Quinn to understand how limited her freedom was?

Her irritation flared into a slow simmer. She was tired of minimizing her brother's arrogance, tired of being reprimanded or forced to listen to his small-minded, uninformed opinions.

After offering her brother and nephew a hurried goodbye, she took a deep breath. She didn't exhale until Morgan had closed the front door behind him.

"Damn," she spoke in a near whisper. "I'll never please that man."

"Is that so important?" Quinn was standing behind her, speaking in that mesmerizing tone he used so well. She felt his fingers resting lightly on her shoulders. His hands dropped to her waist. As she took another cleansing breath and exhaled it, Kali leaned back against his chest.

"You have this horrible habit, Quinn. Persistence."

"Hmmm. I call it decisiveness. And it's not a habit. It's part of me, a deep character flaw you'll find impossible to ignore. How about another picnic tonight at sunset?"

He was a man who liked challenges. Kali remembered the words he'd spoken the night before. She stepped away, then turned to face him. "Do you really think you can tempt me away from my work whenever you feel like it?"

"Absolutely." He was smiling rakishly. "I'll be your guide to adventure. Admit it. You've been waiting for someone like me all your life, Kali, someone to show you the beauty right outside your own window."

"In a few months, *your* new house will be right outside my window. I'm too busy for any of this, Quinn. My work, the land, the research—they all come first in my life."

"I'm not convinced of that, Kali." Quinn began moving toward the door, gathering his hat and shaving kit on the way. "But you're right about me being persistent. I'll bring food for tonight's picnic. My motor home will be here by then. Just knock on the door."

Four

——

Thoughts of Kali swept through his mind as Quinn stepped into the chilly waters of the Columbia River. For a moment, he thought he'd inhaled the sweet scent of blossoms from her orchards. But that was impossible. His nostrils were filled with the wind that lashed westward, buffeting the eastbound river current that swirled around his board.

Glancing up, he acknowledged the wave from his sailing partner, Jack. For safety's sake, he never entered the water without a buddy.

Taking a deep refreshing breath, he willed all thoughts and images of Kali from his mind. This sport commanded his full attention. Pushing the crimson sail up, Quinn caught the unfailing breeze and rose from the water, front arm extended, his hands taut on the boom.

A surge of excitement rippled through him as he leaned his body back trustingly close to the water and felt the board knife through the whitecaps. Licking along at speeds of thirty to thirty-five miles an hour, he began to jibe back and forth in a zigzag pattern. After twenty minutes of good workout, the tension that had been building all morning began to ease.

Challenging nature had always held a fascination for Quinn. Even as a teenager he loved to test himself, to go just beyond his limits. The freedom and challenge of surfing, and later boardsailing, had given him a release from his father's regimented lifestyle. A lifestyle Quinn felt obliged to adopt after business school when he joined his father's food-processing firm.

Five years later it was evident there wouldn't be a Sullivan "and Son." Quinn had risen in the ranks, progressing from production foreman to warehouse manager to administrative service and sales. But his innovative ideas were rejected. Hopes of working harmoniously with his father diminished when his proposal for a line of natural fruit-flavored ice cream was turned down without review.

Despite his father's efforts to mold him, Quinn's rebellious streak remained evident. He resigned from the family business and caught the next wind to Australia.

The months that followed were jumbled in his memory. He'd competed in boardsailing events around the world. Until Maui. It was there he realized winning had become everything for him. He was exhibiting the very traits he'd come to hate in his father. Stay on top. Be aggressive. Never give an inch.

The work ethic had no boundaries for his father. The man had given up all leisure time activities to pursue financial gain. He lived to work. For Quinn, the boundaries had been blurred, blending with his pursuit of the perfect boardsailing conditions, the perfect slalom, the perfect wave. The sport he loved so much had become a profession that obsessed his every waking hour.

Quinn had left Maui dazed by this realization. Soon after, he harnessed his competitive drive and directed it into establishing his own ice cream company in Australia, Queensland Ice. He learned to forgive himself, give his best in every endeavor but not to expect perfection. He challenged himself to purposely take time for life's small pleasures.

Pleasures like a picnic on the ridge at sunset.

Pleasures Kali thought frivolous. That's what frightened him. Kali was consumed by her work and showed no signs of relenting.

For the past month, she'd turned down his invitations to any leisure activity that required more than an hour of her time. They'd shared less than half a dozen romantic picnics on the cliff. While construction on his house progressed, there was little change in her cautious approach to their growing relationship.

Quinn forced himself to focus on the sail. He had allowed his mind to dwell on his problems with Kali too often. Like so many things in life, if he just relaxed, the answers would come to him.

He smiled to himself. The moment he anticipated had arrived, a oneness with wind and water and the invisible force at his back. Didn't he need to feel the same synchronicity with Kali? Was the harmonious blending of two diverse minds possible?

He couldn't resist a challenge, and at the moment, Kali Rainwater was a puzzle worth pursuing. Was she simply as changeable as the wind that had made the gorge a boardsailor's paradise? Or was Kali as set in her ways as the immovable stone cliffs that gave this area its beauty?

Shading her eyes from the bright April sun, Kali stood near the edge of the ridge and studied the colorful armada of boardsailors on the river far below, searching for Quinn's distinctive crimson sail and multicolored dry suit. She spotted him within seconds, gracefully crisscrossing the water like a gladiator guiding his chariot.

He was a born risk taker. She could see that in him now and found the thought a little frightening—a free-spirited man who didn't give up easily. What possessed him to risk pursuing her friendship when the odds were so low?

Quinn was a frequent visitor on her land, full of inquiries about the orchards, curious about her breeding projects and asking altogether too many questions about her.

But that didn't perturb her as much as the picnics at sunset. With his easy smile and windswept hair, he'd weakened her defenses. At his encouragement she'd sampled sushi, sashimi, and sun-dried tomatoes . . . and loved them all. There was something very sensual about the way he moved the chopsticks towards her mouth to offer her the last piece of raw fish—*Hamachi*. But an entire shipload of *ika*, *maguro*, and *saba* wouldn't change the situation.

The problem was simple. They were totally wrong for each other. He was drawn to the wilder elements of water and wind. She was tied to the stability of her land. He trusted fate. She trusted her instincts. Quinn was rootless, a half-a-year-man. She was anchored to tradition and family duty.

Repeatedly, and with methodical precision, she'd mentally outlined their differences for the past month, but the outcome was always the same. She was still intrigued with Quinn Sullivan.

Kali withdrew a crumpled note from her pocket and read it for the third time. Quinn was inviting her to a full day of sight-seeing in the nearby countryside. As if he would conduct the tour and she'd be his guest. She was the native and he was the alien! She was tempted to go along with his plan just to show off her vast knowledge of the Hood River Valley.

But something deep within tugged at her. It had been years since she'd driven down the scenic highway with her mind on the Valley's picture-perfect beauty. She was too busy calculating crop yields and increased productivity. Quinn was giving her the chance to play tourist. What better guide could she have? Judging from his frequent absences from the motor home, the man had been playing tourist since his arrival.

Kali toyed with the long braid that hung over her shoulder. April and May were frantic months. Planting, spraying, the Blossom Festival, gopher baiting, mowing . . . the list was endless. And she didn't have a foreman this year. Her schedule was almost doubled, leaving little time for her research project. How could she possibly find the hours for lazy picnics and long drives in the country?

She stepped closer to the ridge and followed Quinn's bloodred sail with her eyes. Rising and falling rhythmically, the sail had a hypnotic effect. Much like the man.

"All right. I'll take your scenic tour, Mr. Sullivan," she whispered to the wind.

"Why are you laughing? I'm simply giving a brief history of all these waterfalls," Quinn demanded in a voice filled with mirth.

"Correction. You're *rewriting* the history of the Columbia River Scenic Highway and you won't let me correct you on anything!" Kali's words were lost in the wind as Quinn maneuvered the Jeep around another winding curve in the ancient stone-lined roadway. She snuck a sidelong glance at the impressive man at the wheel. They'd spent the morning visiting the seven waterfalls that dotted the twenty-two mile stretch of two-lane highway.

"I love it when you laugh, Grasshopper." Quinn reached over and placed a hand on her jeans-clad thigh. "It's contagious—like that smile you keep hidden. I hope to see it more often. Especially today."

His reference to her appearance as a grasshopper in the St. Uhro Day parade brought an instant flood of warmth. She recalled the magic moment they'd danced together, the moment the magic had begun for her.

Abandoning her diminutive glance, Kali chose to turn fully to stare at Quinn. The light shining through the latticework of leaves overhead dappled his face with sunshine and shadow, emphasizing his masculine profile and the gleam of his smile.

When had he become so irresistibly attractive? Kali pondered. A gossamer web of intimacy had been steadily woven between them since he'd appeared on her doorstep at dawn. He was dressed in blue jeans and a sweatshirt so stylish it instantly marked him as an outsider to her small community. The soft teal fabric captured her attention as it defined his well-muscled chest and the powerful set of his shoulders.

Faded denim and an "aw shucks" smile added to his boy-next-door-who's-been-around-the-world mystique. He was a chameleon, confident in any situation, and Kali envied that in her new neighbor.

"I meant 'Grasshopper' as an endearment, Kali." Quinn returned her glance, fixing her with eyes the color of sapphires. "I hope you don't mind."

"I know. And I like it."

"Good. Why don't we steer this historical tour over to some area of grass where we can open up that picnic basket. I'm starving."

Kali directed him to Rooster Rock State Park where sunbathers were divided into clothed and unclothed beaches on the Columbia River. She suggested they picnic at one end of the park that offered a secluded cove of low-lying trees and calming waterfront.

Half an hour later, Kali lowered her forkful of chilled Chinese chicken salad and thought of a tactful way to react to his latest revelation. "Are you serious, Quinn? You make ice cream for a living?"

"Not just any ice cream. Queensland Ice. We produce sorbets and fruit-flavored quality ice creams—"

"You sound like a commercial. I remember you saying you were involved in marketing surveys for food production—but ice cream?"

"Why does that surprise you so much?"

"It sounds like fun. Almost too much fun."

"You might be right. Work can seem like play if you really enjoy it. My partner and I had tremendous success in Australia, and now we're planning to duplicate that here in the States."

"And what happens if you fail?"

"Fail?" Quinn looked as if she'd spoken in a foreign language. "The thought never occurred to me."

"You seem to be addicted to taking risks, Mr. Sullivan. The boardsailing, the carefree travel and starting new businesses."

"Everything in life is a risk, Kali. I can't imagine a time when I'll stop accepting the challenge of what waits for me beyond the bend."

Kali felt a twist in her stomach. "That makes us opposites. I'm more likely to ask for a diagram of the bend, complete with topographical maps."

"Come on, Kali. Isn't your research a risk?"

"My special strawberry is a goal, not a risk. Anyway, I guess I'm just waiting for the day when everything feels secure—home, land, income, personal life."

"Sounds like boredom to me," Quinn said with a chuckle. "You see security as some kind of accomplishment?"

"It's not boredom or security. It's more like tranquility. I guess I see tranquility as a form of freedom."

"What if that freedom is threatened every time your tranquility is broken? I think of life as a series of waves. You can't stop the waves but you can learn to surf through the turmoil."

Kali turned to look beyond the isolated cove to the broad Columbia. Whitecaps flecked the green-gray surface of the river. Why was she suddenly more open to what Quinn was saying? He wasn't some two-bit philosopher offering psychobabble and trendy advice. Quinn lived what he believed. And what was she doing? Living in fear of taking a chance with a relationship?

Kali felt a giving, a relaxing of some inner guard. Perhaps it was time to let go just a little.

As she leaned back on the blanket, she looked down at the soft pink fabric of her top. One of the buttons on the yoke neck had fallen open, exposing a glimpse of her lacy bra. She looked up to find Quinn's warm gaze on her.

"You're relaxing, Grasshopper," he said softly. "Maybe you're learning to surf."

"I don't know. Maybe I'm just giving the idea some consideration," Kali whispered. She began to pack up the remains of their picnic.

* * *

"I can understand why you keep referring to this land as your pride and joy," Quinn spoke with awe as he surveyed the Rainwater acreage hours later. He'd suggested their scenic drive through the valley of blossoming fruit conclude with a tour of Kali's orchards.

"My heritage," Kali answered simply, her expression suddenly faraway. "It seems to have taken over my whole life. I wake up listing chores and fall asleep regretting the things I didn't have time for."

"Leisure activities?"

"Nothing as exotic as that," she laughed in response. "I'm talking about simple things. Sitting down for half an hour with a cup of coffee and my cat and doing absolutely nothing. Listening to music. Driving in the country, Quinn, like we did today. Taking time for myself."

"Isn't that what today is all about?"

"I guess I still think of leisure time as a reward for hard work. I'll probably feel guilty for weeks about taking a whole day off like this."

"What exactly is a day like this?"

"Being with you, Quinn. Learning more about you, peeling away a few of those mysterious layers."

"So you know all my secrets now. Do I still intrigue you, Kali?"

"Yes—" She paused, but her eyes reflected warmth and humor. "Yes, you do."

"And you intrigue me more than ever, Kali," Quinn said with a whisper, taking her in his arms. He moved his fingers up to trace the line of her jaw from her ear to the stubborn tilt of her chin.

They'd shared kisses during their picnics at sunset on the ridge, but never had she looked more beautiful to him. In the hues of early evening, the pink of her low-necked top gave her dark skin a shimmering glow.

"Kiss me, Quinn." Her fingers moved up to rest on his shoulders as he bent to cover her half-parted mouth with his.

A strong east breeze ruffled through the boughs overhead, showering them with a cascade of pale pink apple blossoms. As the kiss deepened, Quinn felt Kali's firm breasts pressing against his chest, felt his own body responding to every sensation. The sweet scent of apple blossoms mingled with her herbal shampoo, the warmth of her mouth offset the cool evening breeze that swept against his back.

His hand slipped down, moving over the soft fabric to the swell of her breast. One button and then another fell open at the press of his fingers. He brushed the folds aside to tease a fingertip along the lace of her bra. A second shower of petals whispered downward.

With gentle movements, Quinn gathered a handful of blossoms from Kali's hair and shoulders and released them so the pale pink petals drifted between the glimmering satin of her breasts.

"You're beautiful, Kali," he whispered hoarsely as his fingers eased the lace aside. He heard her soft intake of breath as he blew the petals from the valley between her breasts. Bending down, he pressed his lips against the exposed fullness.

Kali moaned against the onslaught of emotion. The tapestry of intimacy that had been woven between them all day was rich with color and texture and something far more important. Trust.

Though her thoughts were focused on the movement of Quinn's hands and lips and the pleasure they brought, Kali felt the pleasure doubled by the lifting of old doubts. And just as quickly, she felt the weight of old concerns left unaddressed press down on her, and the pleasure began to slowly dissipate.

"Quinn," she spoke against the muscled column of his neck. "Please." Kali stepped back, adjusting her bra as she moved uneasily in his embrace.

"What is it? Guilt pangs?" Quinn spoke softly in a controlled voice, but it was obvious he was unable to mask his frustration. Kali felt the tension in his forearms and watched a muscle twitch along his jawline while he waited for her answer.

"We talked about goals and risks earlier today. I-I know you understand the desire for success with your American plant for Queensland Ice and—"

"What are you getting at, Kali?"

"My strawberry. I've made it sound so easy, so simplistic, but it's more complicated than that, Quinn. I've dreamed of developing a drought-resistant variety since California had the drought in 1977. When my father had the stroke and I quit college to take over his land, I vowed to keep that dream alive."

"Calm down," he whispered as he tightened his embrace and moved his hand in great soothing strokes over her back.

"But you have to understand. The big researchers have all the money and technology they need to succeed. I'm not going to give you a lesson in crossbreeding or biotechnology or advanced genetics, Quinn, but this is the last year I can afford to pursue this goal."

"And you think I might interfere, right?"

"I wasn't going to put it quite so bluntly." Kali smiled and moved her arms around him.

"How would you phrase it then, Grasshopper?"

The endearment tore at her heart. Had she destroyed the trust and intimacy this special day had brought?

"I'd have to say I'm simply not sure if there's room in my life for success and a relationship." Kali closed her eyes against the dilemma she faced. She was one researcher, a woman who'd never finished her degree and felt a keen sense of family loyalty to the multigenerational land. She couldn't begin to compete with the large research firms that had made so many recent strides.

Maybe Quinn was an excuse. If she had a relationship and her research project faltered, she could blame the distraction. She could blame the presence of a man in her life rather than face whatever truth she needed to confront.

Perhaps it was guilt about his poor health that drove her father to insist she continue her breeding projects while working the land. He'd always said "a Rainwater always finishes what they start." Did that apply to goals that turned your life upside down and made you cautious about giving and receiving love?

She looked up into the dark blue of Quinn's expectant gaze. She couldn't tell him everything, but she could describe her emotions.

Kali eased out of his arms, choosing to stand apart for the moment.

"I've let down my guard for you, Quinn, and I rarely do that for anyone—even myself. I know boardsailing is your chosen area of expertise, but I feel like a bit of a wind dancer myself." She looked back at him and smiled. "I've walked these orchards, played on the ridge and explored the gorge since childhood. I'm not talking about the gorge winds that blow through here." She let her smile fade.

"The winds I'm referring to are the legacy of land I've inherited, my father's stroke and the memory of his harsh lessons, and the vows I made to him. I sometimes think Morgan believes it's his duty as my brother to continuously remind me of those promises. Maybe the worst part is my willingness to let all these elements move me—"

"You're describing a rag doll. A dancer has strength, Kali. I saw it in you the day we met. It drew me to you in the beginning, and your strength is there now, whether you reach your goal of the perfect strawberry or not. You don't need me to tell you that."

A brisk breeze blew through the canopy of blossoms overhead. The soft petals swirled around them, shimmering in the beginning hues of sunset.

As Kali made a brief attempt to brush the blossoms from her hair, Quinn captured her mouth in a kiss.

"Let me be a bold new wind for you, Kali," he spoke against the edge of her mouth. "A wind that shares and strengthens your dance."

Five

Twenty minutes, Aunt Kali. We can watch the boardheads for twenty minutes then rush through the rest of your errands," Travis pleaded a second time as the truck neared Hood River's marina park.

Kali glanced up from her list of supplies to scan the riverfront. She was immediately assaulted by the shock of Day-Glo colors and the glint of the midday sun. Out on the Columbia, dozens of boardsailors raced through the water.

"I'm going to have to rush through the errands as it is, Travis, and then we have to check the—hey!"

Her nephew pulled sharply into the marina's parking lot before she could finish her sentence.

"Quinn's out there today. See the kangaroo on his sail and the—"

"Stop the truck, Travis," Kali ordered in a tone she hadn't used with the fifteen-year-old since he set off the frost alarms intentionally two years earlier.

Scowling fiercely, the boy brought the Ford to an abrupt stop.

"Turn the engine off and trade places with me," Kali continued using the same cool, forceful tone. When Travis didn't budge from the driver's seat, she felt anger and hurt. Travis had never deliberately defied her before. Where had her friendly little tagalong disappeared to? Was he going to be replaced by this sullen brooding boy-man?

Exhaling slowly, Kali turned her body toward him. "You've got a little time before you get your license, but you should know by now you don't swerve across a highway like that."

"I thought you wanted to see Quinn as much as I did."

"What has that got to do with safe driving?"

"Why are you upset? Dad drives the same way, and I didn't hurt anybody. You want me to drive like a wimp?"

"What's gotten into you lately? All you want to do is come down here and watch the wind smurfs and hang out downtown. You've got responsibilities at home to think about, Travis. Your Dad can't run the orchards by himself."

"He's got a foreman and the crews. He doesn't need me except to tell me what I'm doing wrong all the time. I don't care about spraying and gopher baiting and crawling out of bed in the middle of the night when the frost alarms go off."

Slumping down in the seat, he laid his head back and stared at the ceiling of the cab. "None of that stuff interests me. Anyone could do it."

"What *does* interest you?"

"Right now?" Travis gave her a sidelong glance.

"This month. This week. Today. Right this minute. What do you care about?"

"You don't have to get dramatic on me, Kali. I still care about school and the usual things, but lately I feel like coming down here and watching the boardsailors. I guess I do it a lot. Thinking about the way they look at life makes me feel good."

"Maybe that's a bit of a generalization. These people can't all have the same attitude about life."

"Sure they do, Kali. I figured it out. They wouldn't be out there taking risks and having a good time if they didn't have the courage. They're not afraid of anything. Some of them don't know where they'll be living six months from now."

"Don't you think it takes courage to plant orchards and chance everything you own against the whims of nature? Those boardsailors are pitting their bodies against wind and water and I admire them. But I'm in my orchards battling the same damn elements and more. It takes courage to do both, Travis."

Her words faltered. Travis's narrow view had fanned her slowly simmering anger to a boiling point. Kali unclenched her fists and took a deep breath.

Oddly enough, what Travis was saying sounded vaguely familiar. She'd been having similar thoughts since Quinn had announced his intent to teach her to boardsail when her schedule slowed down. Somewhere in the back of her mind, she clung to the thought that learning Quinn's adventurous sport would change her. She'd be less earthbound, able to let go of her cares and enjoy each day fully.

"Travis, do you think buying a board and rig and learning to boardsail is going to give you a sudden dose of this courage?"

"I got it all planned out. I heard Quinn Sullivan's almost ready to start hiring boardsailors to work in his new ice cream plant. It'll be great. A coupla guys said the plant will have wind clauses. When the wind comes up, the workers can take their time off. It's the perfect job for me."

"You have a job, helping your father."

"I can make more money working for Quinn, and I won't get hassled."

"Maybe you need to be hassled a little bit. What happened to your sense of responsibility, your pride in the family orchards, Travis? If you don't help out, your father will have to hire an extra hand."

Kali was struck by a flash of déjà vu. Her father had preached the same refrain when she was sixteen and announced her plans to work after school for "real money."

"Man, no one understands. Things are just different for me now. Why should I do work that doesn't interest me?" Her nephew had turned to stare at the bright sails on the water and the tanned healthy-looking people enjoying the spring sunshine.

How could orchardists in jeans and flannel shirts compete with this idyllic carefree scene? Kali wondered if the hard-work ethic of sacrifice at any cost was the kind of legacy she wanted to pass on to the children she hoped to have someday.

On the other hand, how could she completely disregard the lessons passed on from her father and the grandparents she loved so dearly? They passed on their love of the land, their respect for all living things, and her Chinook heritage. Yet, like Travis, she was intrigued by Quinn's rootless wanderings and his freedom from family obligation. Perhaps legacies had price tags. High price tags.

She set her list of errands on the truck's dashboard. The relationship between Morgan and Quinn was tense enough without adding this twist. Travis's obvious adoration of their boardsailing neighbor had already set Morgan's teeth on edge. The two men lived on adjoining land, but the tone of their relationship had been set that first meeting in her kitchen. Morgan remained cool and aloof, if not surly, in Quinn's presence. And Quinn danced his way around the tense confrontations with practiced ease which only made matters worse.

She was taking more time for Quinn and it felt right. Slowly she was finding herself imbued with new energy. The work hadn't changed—there was always too much of it. But the resentment that made the load feel so heavy had softened slightly. And she no longer questioned the right or wrong of enjoying the company of an attractive man.

The sight of bright sails on the water relaxed her. For a moment she forgot about Morgan and Travis and family matters. She felt a twinge of guilt as she studied Travis's proud profile. How could she help her nephew work out the age-old dilemma faced by children whose parents expect them to work in a family business?

Travis knew little of the gentling effect of a woman in the home. Morgan's wife had died two years after Travis was born. Morgan's grief was added to the many resentments he'd built over the years. Kali didn't want Travis to reflect his father's sullen ungiving nature. If only she could find a way to explain family loyalty without alienating the boy.

"I'm sorry, Kali," Travis mumbled while he kept his attention transfixed on the riverfront. "Pulling in here like that was stupid. I guess I wanted you to know how important it is to me. Maybe I thought you'd enjoy seeing Quinn. I can't remember you spending so much time with a man before—"

"I care a great deal about Quinn but—" Kali touched the edge of his sleeve "—I think we need to talk about your sudden interest in boardsailing and how it might affect your home life. Does Morgan know how you feel?"

"He knows I spend time down here, but Dad doesn't know I applied for a job at Queensland Ice."

"I don't suggest you surprise him by leaving him a note the day you start work this summer."

"First I have to ask him to help me buy a board and sail and the other gear."

Kali couldn't suppress a nervous laugh. Quinn was going to turn out looking absolutely villainous in Morgan's eyes. She would have to give Travis a few lessons in the fine art of waiting for the right time and the right place to approach her brother about spending money on an expensive sport.

"Come on, Travis. Start the engine. We'll continue this conversation while we run our errands. If there's time left over, we'll grab a small pizza and come back here. I think it might be worth my time today to tell you how I went through very similar problems at about your age."

"And you're going to teach me how to solve them, right?" Travis looked at her with an expectant smile.

"Well..." Kali chuckled as she picked up her list from the dashboard. Had she ever found the answers? Would she in the future, or would she help to further the hard-work ethic so inherent in their lifestyles?

"Actually, Travis, I never found a solution, but I survived my teenage years."

"And you want to give *me* advice?"

"Maybe. Who knows? I still have feelings about what happened back then and what's happening now. Maybe we can just share feelings."

"Feelings? Ugghh." Travis grimaced. "You know, one of the things I always liked about you, Kali, was knowing you weren't one of those 'touchy-feely' types as Dad calls 'em. You don't fuss over things and you don't get overly emotional. You're just folks, Kali. You know, down-to-earth. Don't go changin' on me now, okay?"

"I resent that, Travis. You make me sound like an emotionless robot."

"Robots can't eat pizza. Does that mean I get the whole thing?"

"This very human aunt will be glad to split the pizza equally."

Quinn slowed his stride as the hiking path changed from an open rocky area into heavy vegetation. The yellow-green leaves filtered the bright sky above into an Alice-in-Wonderland magic alcove, making him pause to catch his breath.

"Kali," Quinn called her name softly. "Please, stop right there...before the next switchback. Turn around and let me look at you in this light."

She turned slightly, her brows raised as if to question his sanity, her mouth widening into a playful smile. "If I keep stopping like this, we'll never finish the hike to Angel's Rest."

Quinn ignored her comment, choosing instead to take in the scene. He loved her luminous dark eyes and glowing skin, the glorious way the mystical light accentuated her high cheekbones and drew his eyes downward to her mouth. Her laughing mouth.

"You look positively moonstruck, Mr. Sullivan, and it's the middle of the day. Even if it were night, I'm sure the moon is waning."

"It can't be. Not when I feel like this." Catching up with her, Quinn slipped his hand around her waist and drew her close. "I can't seem to get enough of you, Kali."

"You're already taking up every minute I can spare."

"I'm sorry to be so greedy but I want your days and, more than ever, Grasshopper, I want your nights." He brushed his lips across her cheek. "I want to lie beside you in that big beautiful bed of yours and do glorious things to you."

"Quinn, there are other hikers on the trail." She danced out of his arms, her cheeks flushed with color.

He felt the tightness in his chest grow into an ache. "Come back into the light," Quinn urged.

She shook her head. "There's more light up ahead, Quinn, and I'm sure it comes from the same source. Besides, you see one hiking trail, you've seen 'em all."

"Cynic. I've been on hiking trails around the world and nothing compares to where I am at the moment, and whom I'm with. We've met for a reason, Kali. Call it destiny."

"Sorry. I don't believe in that kind of fate." She turned away from him to head up the next switch-back.

"I didn't know fate came in two flavors."

"Sure, ice cream man," she said with a laugh. "Some people believe things are predetermined. They call it destiny, karma, or the wheel of fortune, futures written in the stars. Maybe I'm wrong, but I don't find that thought romantic."

"Not romantic?" Quinn caught her from behind and imprisoned her gently in his arms. "Kali, what could be more romantic than me being destined to meet you, destined to walk this trail to Angel's Rest with you, destined to make love to you on moonlit sheets."

"You really are moonstruck." Again she laughed and wiggled out of his embrace. As she backed away from him, her tennis shoes catching in the heavy coating of pine needles on the path, her smile faded.

"I guess I don't want to think it might be my destiny to be this happy for only a little while. That sounds crazy, doesn't it?"

"Absurd. Don't you trust your feelings for me?"

"Maybe I feel a little overwhelmed by your background. You've been everywhere. My dates were limited to college boys, and when I came back to Hood River, I dated locals a bit. Nothing as exotic as Australia or—"

"If you think a scarred passport makes a person more capable of holding my interest, you're wrong. And I'll show you how wrong you are when we get back to Rainwater Ridge."

Kali paused at the edge of the path. Mention of passports and faraway places reminded her of the dilemma that faced her. She'd allowed the weeks of growing intimacy to fog the issue. Quinn was a rootless wanderer, while she was a woman whose past and future were firmly rooted on family land. And how could she continue to ignore the simple fact that this man had purchased her prime piece of property?

"We'd get home sooner *if* we turned around now, Kali."

She looked up and slowly absorbed the meaning of his comment.

"Kali, didn't you say it was a two-mile hike?"

"It isn't far," she stammered, pushing thoughts of property aside.

"I'm not complaining. I'm enjoying it, especially the moments when you let me catch up with you." Weaving his fingers through her hair, he bent her head back slightly and kissed her fully on the mouth. "Why don't we just find a nice secluded meadow, a flat one with tall grass.''

''Angel's Rest is flat.'' She felt caught in his web again.

''And public. I thought grasshoppers enjoyed hiding in tall grass.'' He spoke against the edge of her mouth. ''Why don't we start looking?''

''Because a Rainwater always finishes a hike?'' Kali attempted a return to their original plan.

With a smile he dropped his hands to her shoulders and stepped back. ''You have a few hundred years of family tradition to call on whenever it's convenient, don't you?''

''Does it bother you, Quinn, that I have deep family roots?'' she ventured. ''I mean, you hardly mention your parents or your sister.''

''I put that behind me long ago when I realized nothing I did or would ever do could please my father. So I seem to develop surrogate families wherever I go. Suits me fine, too. My family was judgmental, and the anger that existed between us didn't help anyone.''

''But the wandering...do you feel it's coming to an end?''

Quinn's gaze softened as he studied her expression. ''I thought you understood. When the boardsailing season is over here, I'll be heading back to Australia and leaving management of the North American plant to a capable team. But I'll be here for at least six months out of the year.''

Having her time with Quinn narrowed down to numbers left Kali feeling suddenly detached from the warmth that had been building between them during the hike.

"I have to admit I envy you a bit," Quinn continued, "living on your family's land and working the old soil like you do. It's a nice thought, passing on things from generation to generation. Being in one place. I like continuity."

As they walked on toward Angel's Rest, the issue of Quinn's wanderlust grew heavier on her mind. His dream house on the ridge property would be completed soon. Her dream had been altered to focus on buying back the land she'd been forced to give up last year. How far was she willing to go to keep her vow to her father?

How could she trust her feelings fully? Was part of her attraction to Quinn the fact that he possessed a vital part of her past?

"Quinn, I think it's time you visited my office and greenhouse," she broke the silence with her announcement. "Tonight. I'll try to explain the high cost of continuity."

Six

I wish I had something comforting and eloquent and intelligent to say right now." Quinn ran his fingers through his hair, straightened his back and looked up from the accumulation of data on Kali's desk. "I'm sorry, Kali. I'm no expert on plant breeding, but even I can see how this new article confirms your suspicions."

She'd been tense and preoccupied when he arrived earlier that evening. After a brief tour of the seedling fields and greenhouse, she'd taken him to her office and explained the problem she faced as a single researcher competing with large-scale breeding projects and state-funded studies. She'd offered him a few articles from professional journals and newspapers, with specific areas highlighted to prove her point further.

Then she'd handed him the journal that had arrived in the afternoon mail.

The sad truth was that Kali's research on drought-resistant strawberries was now obsolete because of the recent findings of a large California firm.

"I'm the one who doesn't believe in destiny. Why is it I get this kind of news in the mail the day I invite you into my little sanctuary?" Kali pushed her chair back from her computer terminal. "I wanted you to know what was involved in my work but I-I never expected to have to sit here and tell you I've failed."

"Kali, I'm glad it happened this way—" he tried to interject. She appeared oblivious to his attempt.

"I talked myself into believing I could do the work of ten people in less time than required. To say I wasn't being realistic is an understatement, but then this particular berry has been my goal for six years. Six years." She paused and looked at him in silence. "It's going to be hard to abandon my dream."

Quinn longed to reach out and console her, but there was something in her body language that warned against it. She was revealing yet another side to him tonight. Like a finely tempered blade, she was strengthened by adversity, challenged by the impossible.

"Didn't you say it was also your father's goal for you?" he asked when she paused. "Is this what you meant when you referred to the high cost of family continuity?"

"I don't want to blame my own misjudgment entirely on my father, Quinn. He believed in me, and there's no shame in that." She turned off the computer and brushed the loose hair back from her face with a distracted motion. "I promised to succeed in this experiment, and instead I failed, but it's not because I didn't try.

"Maybe I've used that foolish vow as a part of my denial," she added. "And I almost used you as an excuse as well."

"I don't understand." He hooked his arm over the back of the chair.

"I told you I didn't have time in my life for both success and a relationship. Some part of me is tempted to blame my failure with the drought project on you— Quinn the distraction. But that wouldn't be fair. You haven't distracted me that much—yet."

As he rose from the chair, Quinn smiled and placed a hand over his heart. "I'm insulted. Here I thought I was a major distraction from the moment I hit town."

"Thanks for teasing me," she responded with a choking laugh. She stood and turned off the lamp over the terminal. "This meant so much to me. It's a wonder I don't feel more devastated, isn't it? Come on, I'm going to pick a few test berries in the seedling fields then check on some equipment in the greenhouse."

He followed her to the office door. "I don't want you to think I'm taking your problem lightly. Frankly, I'm surprised, too. I figured you'd be far more upset, Kali."

"It's strange, I almost feel relieved. It isn't the end of the world. People go through disappointment every day and manage to survive to try something new. And I'm fortunate I have another breeding project to fall back on." They walked the breezeway between the office and the greenhouse. "The second project's closer to my heart, actually."

"Another strawberry?"

"Uh-huh. Grandma Rainwater had a secret patch of berries she showed me when I was old enough to help her pick them. These were special, always extra sweet. Of course, taste was all I cared about at that age.

"But later I noticed they were large and firm and plump, a brilliant red and, well, I had the good sense to see what I had. I crossbred with another reliable variety, and after a few years of playing with cultivars and seedling fields I was able to make the berry more productive."

"And what did your father say about this project, or does it matter?"

"He thought the drought-resistant berry was more socially significant, but you're right. It doesn't matter now, does it? I think if my father were around right now, he'd be happy about the success I've had with Grandma's project."

Kali picked up a clipboard. "I'll just be a few minutes," she said politely. She soon busied herself, explaining as she jotted down figures and checked the progress of the breeding projects in the greenhouse.

Quinn watched with wonder as she quickly became absorbed in her tasks. Ten minutes later, she set the clipboard aside and dimmed the overhead lights.

"It's a bit ethereal in here," he noted from his vantage point in one corner. "Do you ever forget about time and space and get lost?"

"Lost in space or lost in my work?" She raised her brows then began walking toward him. "A little of both, maybe. I'm usually so tired at night that I sometimes resort to misting myself to stay awake."

"Sounds like fun. We could try doing that together. Now, perhaps."

"Quinn, I have to admit you're persistent."

"So, Grasshopper, you still have reasons to spend hours in your greenhouse?" He tried to mask his disappointment.

"I'm afraid so. I have to think about my financial losses and recoup what I can. And I'm sure I will. You see, Grandma's berry's high in natural sugar content so it'd be useful in recipes sweetened with fruit juices. With a health-conscious country, my timing might be right on the money."

"I get the impression you're not really in this for the money," he observed as she moved into his arms. "Am I right?"

"I'm a businesswoman. Do you think I'm going to be foolish enough to say a profit isn't important? We may have to do business together again in the future."

"Speaking of the future, look up," Quinn whispered as he coaxed her chin upward with the touch of a finger. "The stars are shimmering. You can see them through the glass roof. They don't look real . . . I suspect you might have simply painted them up there." Quinn looked down at Kali's eyes. "But that wouldn't explain why they're reflected in your eyes. You look radiant. Must be all those hours you spend outdoors."

"Don't forget the misting."

"If that's a Rainwater beauty secret, I'm willing to do a testimonial." Taking her delicate heart-shaped face between his palms, he gently kissed the corner of each eye, smiling when he felt the sweep of her eyelashes against his upper lip. "Here's to future success."

"I think it's time I celebrated the success I had months ago with Grandma's cultivar. I didn't really feel any joy when I filed for a patent."

"A patent? Like an inventor?"

"Uh-huh. Breeders get a portion of the royalties."

"Now you sound like an author."

"Whoever propagates my cultivar—my new variety of strawberry—has to pay a royalty. So I applied to the patent office months ago, and I'm still waiting to hear from them. But it doesn't matter at the moment. This experience has helped me grow. I've realized I was so emotionally tied up with the drought project and searching for my father's approval from the beyond that I ignored my own success. Maybe that was an important lesson for me to learn."

"And now you want to celebrate with me?"

"Yes. I'm going to pluck a few berries for taste testing. It's one of the fringe benefits of my work." She put a finger to his lips. "Care to taste the fruit of my labors?"

"Which labor—drought berry or sweet berry?"

She laughed. "Drought berry sounds like a marketing director's nightmare. I'll be right back with the berries closest to my heart, the one you choose to call sweet berry."

Taking a flashlight, she led him outside to one of the fields that stretched beyond and beside the greenhouse area. "As you can see, a few of these berries are ready for a discriminating palate."

Kali picked two of the large plump strawberries and carried them back into the greenhouse. She rinsed them in one of the sinks with the gentle care of a jeweler handling a precious stone.

When she turned to offer Quinn the larger of the berries, he wished he could preserve the moment forever. The dim lights created a blue-black halo around her head. Her hair swung in a movement as soft, slow and sensual as the smile that formed on her lips. This was the Kali he'd seen in rare moments, when work was done, when she wasn't consumed by financial worries or fear of family opinion.

"Mr. Sullivan, count yourself a lucky man. You are the first person on earth—other than myself—to taste the berry that could rock the world." With that pronouncement, she lowered the strawberry to his mouth.

She held her breath as he bit into the fruit with his even white teeth. Quinn had the sexiest mouth she'd ever encountered.

"Hmmm." Closing his eyes, he moaned his approval before biting the remainder of the berry. "Wow! That's sweet! It's so juicy. Now it's your turn." He took the second berry from her hand. "Open wider."

He ran a finger over her half-parted lips, then replaced the pressure of his fingertip with the stroking of the berry's tip. She chose to eat the fruit with slight even nibbles. The juice coated her lips and pooled over, threatening to run down her chin. "Oops!" she laughed and reached up.

"No, let me catch this," Quinn said, brushing her hand away as he quickly lowered his face to hers. His tongue failed to capture the errant rivulet. Kali lifted her chin to prevent its escape, but the sticky fluid moved down the column of her throat.

"Gravity doesn't discourage me." His tongue trailed over her jawline, rasping over the sensitive skin that lay over her rapidly beating pulse, parting the fabric of her shirt to reach the rise of her collarbone. "You created this berry just for tempting me. Admit it."

The urge to laugh that had been so persistent seconds earlier had died. The movement of Quinn's tongue metamorphosed from a tickling sensation to one of inciting desire.

"We can't take a chance on staining this," Quinn murmured against a patch of skin far too close to her heart.

She'd worn a blue-and-white-striped shirt tucked into faded blue jeans. She'd always had trouble with small buttons, but Quinn seemed more than adept at undoing them. Her breathing quickened as he parted the cotton folds and lovingly licked the last of the runaway nectar from the rise of her breast.

His tongue became a sweet fire devouring any vestige of doubt. It flicked against the scalloped lace edge of her bra, doubling the delicious friction that made her painfully aware of every movement.

"Quinn, please listen," she spoke in a hushed whisper. "This—this is the night. I want you tonight. But not here. Not this way."

She paused, distracted by the continued movement of his wet mouth. She didn't want memories of this night to remain here in her greenhouse mingling with her work. She wanted tonight to be special.

"I want to make love to you, Kali." His voice was a hoarse plea that inflamed her more. "Raw, earthy, passionate love."

"Not here. The greenhouse is *too* earthy."

"And glass houses aren't very private," he added gruffly. "Fine. But if you don't start moving toward the bedroom, I might be foolish enough to turn pirate, lift you off your feet and carry you up the stairs."

Minutes later, Blossom mirrupped her displeasure when Kali picked her up off the spacious four-poster bed and moved the sleepy cat to a chair in the hallway.

Turning, Kali found Quinn lighting the hurricane lamp beside the bed. Though he appeared calm, the match shook in his fingers, and his quick uneven breathing set the flame to dancing in a wild erotic pattern.

When he replaced the glass chimney, the lamp sent out a soft even glow that illuminated his tanned angular features. Kali smiled at the imperfect rise in his nose and felt less anxious about any flaws the subdued light might reveal in herself.

When he turned to look at her, there was nothing subdued about the desire in Quinn's eyes. In one swift sure movement, he reached down and pulled his lightweight polo shirt over his head, leaving his upper torso open to her gaze. The action seemed a daring invitation, a blatant nonverbal communication of his need and a reminder of her own.

The room and its furnishings seemed to evaporate into haze as she became more aware of her trembling body. She'd pictured this moment for so long, but her vision had not included shaking limbs, or feet that were immobilized. The boldness she'd felt in the greenhouse warred with old inhibitions and the fears that had kept her at a distance from her desires since Quinn's arrival.

Boldness won. With deliberate abandon, she unbuttoned her jeans. The denim slipped down her slender thighs and she stepped out of them, her eyes never leaving Quinn's face. Dressed only in bra and panties, and the striped shirt he'd unbuttoned in the greenhouse, she experienced a sweet, ragged victory over her old fears.

Quinn rested his palm on one of the ornately carved posts at the foot of the bed and held his other hand out to her.

She moved forward and slipped her hand in his. Quinn brought it to his lips and kissed the back of her fingers with reverence before he drew her closer.

"You're beautiful, Kali." Releasing her hand, he traced the curve of her cheekbone with his thumb. "So delicate and yet so strong..."

"Hmmm, strong..." Kali echoed, fanning her fingers over his smooth well-muscled chest until she felt his nipples peak against the skin of her palms.

Her own body responded in kind when his fingers feathered down her throat to the opened front of her shirt, easing it off her shoulders until it fell in a flutter to the floor.

Quinn was well familiar with Kali's penchant for lacy underthings, but tonight the effect was riveting, a sweet reminder of her deeply sensual nature, and the promise of new discovery.

Her pale pink satin bra shimmered, reflecting the golden lamplight and drawing his attention to the shadows nestled between her breasts. Softly scented shadows he longed to explore.

Where the satin ended, delicate scalloped lacework began, pale ivory lace that accentuated the natural, dark honeyed tones of her skin.

He looped his arms gently around her neck and kissed her forehead lightly. The undersides of his wrists rested on the top of her shoulders. How often had he laid a hand there or smoothed a fingertip or pressed his mouth against the perfect slope of her shoulder? Quinn closed his eyes, pressed his chin against her temple and relaxed his wrists, taking inventory of the wonderful sensations. Kali's skin was a satin all its own.

He wanted to explore every glorious inch of that satin. But his control was shaken by the tiniest movement of her hands on his chest, the heat of her breath against his throat and, when he closed his eyes, the very thought of loving Kali.

Her hands drifted from his chest, lower to his taut stomach then moved back up, running her fingers over his ribs as she went. The exploration continued as her fingertips memorized the corded muscles of his back and ended at the waistband of his jogging shorts.

Kali's hands slipped below the waist, palming the male contours of his firmly rounded buttocks. She was aware of the movement of Quinn's hands on her back, hurriedly unfastening the dainty strap of the satin bra, releasing her breasts to his smoky gaze.

He tested the weight of her curves with his palms before stroking his thumbs across the pebble-hard tips. Kali stepped back, trembling, when Quinn lowered his head. He circled a dusky nipple with his tongue, drawing dizzying patterns that made her weave her fingers through his hair and arch against the pleasure. He drew the point into his hungry mouth and she moved her hands to Quinn's shoulders as the world fell away.

Then the movements fused into sensations of sharing. All clothing abandoned, they worshipped one another with hands and mouths, with softly spoken words and the touches that trust brings.

Kali moaned and felt her knees weaken as Quinn's pleasuring touch edged to the tops of her thighs. She arched her body against the movement of his fingers, and heard his breathing quicken, paced to the rhythm and tangle of their passion.

"Wet silk," he whispered, continuing the inner stroking, testing her readiness until small ragged moans escaped her throat.

Her fingers curled around him in intimate possession until his moans echoed hers and he uttered a breathless entreaty.

Moving onto the bed, they reached for one another anew.

"I want you, Kali," Quinn whispered, her name more breath than voice. "And that's probably the last intelligible comment I'll make to you because..."

"Because your body says it all," she whispered. "I need you, Quinn. *Now.*"

Kali was suddenly grateful for the short discussion they'd had about protection two days earlier. The intensity of the moment would have made such a discussion impossible.

He poised himself over her, hesitating for half a heartbeat. Then he entered her firmly, gasping with pleasure at the warmth that welcomed him.

They met in a rhythm fused in passion and harmony. Kali closed her eyes against the onslaught of pleasure, wanting to make it last forever but finding the intensity unbearable.

His name tore from her mouth as she soared in chaotic release. Moments later, Quinn echoed her cry of ecstasy.

Kali awoke to daylight, the rasp of a purring cat, the pressure of Blossom's paw on her cheek, and an unmistakably male body aligned to hers from shoulder to knee and then some.

"This cat thinks she's a silent rooster," Kali said with a groan.

"She scratched the door and cried until I let her in," Quinn explained, reaching out to scratch behind Blossom's ear. Then bending over he kissed Kali's bare shoulder. "When it comes to animals and beautiful orchardists, you can call me a softy."

"A softy? Not quite." Kali gave in to the giddiness that pervaded her being. "You forget how closely your body is pressed against mine." She turned to share her smile with him and was rewarded with a sleepy warm hug.

"We were busy all night. Why don't we spend the day in bed?" he suggested.

"Why not? We can ask Blossom to go make breakfast and do our work for us."

"We're both self-employed," Quinn said with a yawn. "I thought people like us had flexible hours, freedom, time on their hands. The work can wait."

"I wish. I think I used up all my flex time yesterday and last night and . . . I don't regret a single moment. But today I have to start irrigation and I haven't finished the spraying and I have to make plans for thinning." She gave a short laughing groan. Curling her fingers through his hair, she brought his mouth back down on hers. "Hmmm. You're right. We should spend the day in bed. Maybe two days."

He wrapped an arm around her waist. His fingers traced the curve of her hip before making broad smoothing motions over her abdomen.

"Careful," Kali warned in a terse whisper. "Blossom is following the movement of your hand and she's getting that wild animal look in her eyes."

"So am I." Quinn let his hand settle just below Kali's breast. "Is this any better?"

"I'm not sure." Her body had been responding to his presence since she awoke. "Now all three of us will have the same certifiable look." She widened her eyes to imitate Blossom and Quinn.

"You know—" he bent to kiss the tip of her nose "—we could still get a few vital things done. Like taste testing the strawberries, again. And I suppose you need to *name* the new berry, Ms. Rainwater."

"Nothing fancy. In my mind, it's always been Grandma Rainwater's berry."

"This is a leading-edge product. To hear you describe it, perhaps one of the many fruits of the future that will revolutionize the way people sweeten their foods." He moved his hand up and began brushing the underside of her breast with his thumb. "Your strawberry needs a name that makes a statement. What kind of statement do you feel like making right now?"

"Maybe this isn't the right time to ask. Something...sensual, perhaps." Kali moaned slightly as Quinn pulled back the coverlet and exposed their upper bodies to cool air and daylight.

"All right," he seemed to enjoy the challenge. "The berry is deep red—crimson, wouldn't you say?"

"Yes."

"And it's shaped like a heart. How about Crimson Heart?"

"Save it for a bestseller. It doesn't say what I want it to say."

"Hmmm, I see."

"I'd like to connect it to the family name because of my grandmother. Something simple like Rainwater Red. What do you think?"

"Rainwater Red? I think it's perfect. I also think it's the perfect time to make love to you, Grasshopper, *after* I put this wild-eyed cat out in the hall."

"Faint of heart?"

"Hardly. My heart has never beat stronger or harder for anyone, Kali. You're making this half-a-year man have strange thoughts about what he might be missing during the rest of the year."

Seven

Kali parked her truck at the now familiar bend in the cemetery roadway where a large oak offered shade from the overhead sun. As she climbed out of the cab, her eyes were drawn upward to the ancient boughs swaying gracefully in the afternoon breeze. Other than the rustling of oak leaves, the hillside was silent, which pleased her. Visiting her father's grave on the anniversary of his death was a private occasion.

She carried two small baskets in her hands but kept her eyes averted from the contents. Her emotions had been through enough roller coaster rides since Quinn returned to Hood River. She wanted this visit to be an island of calm, a chance to come closer to resolving old hurts and revitalizing pleasant memories of her father, Harlan Rainwater.

As she moved toward the site where the majority of the Rainwater family lay in rest, Kali slowed her pace, recognizing the lone male figure standing close to her father's burial plot. Her brother's proud stance and rigid profile were unmistakable.

When Morgan turned, she felt a stab of pain through her chest at the unspoken torment in his deep-set eyes. Why had she selfishly focused on her own grief and never offered her strength to her brother who had suffered as much if not more?

"Two years, Kali. Hard to believe, isn't it?" Morgan greeted her with a nod, speaking in a soft low voice as he walked towards her.

"Seems like forever sometimes, and at other times I still expect him to come running when the frost alarm goes off." Kali touched her hand to Morgan's sleeve. "It's nice that your visit coincided with mine. It never occurred to me to call you and suggest we go to-gether."

"That's all right. I wanted to spend a little time with Katy first."

A second wave of regret washed over Kali. That explained why Morgan's truck wasn't parked at the bend. He'd visited his young wife's grave and walked up to visit their father. Was she so insensitive to believe her brother's normally stoic attitude was impen-etrable?

"What's with the baskets?" Morgan asked after an awkward silence.

"Strawberries—from the breeding projects." Kali hoped her answer would explain everything, but she knew there'd be more questions. Morgan frequently used questions as a defense against any real conversation. She knew because it was an old family habit, one she'd tried hard to break.

The tension between siblings had increased steadily since Quinn's arrival. Why should a visit to a grave site bring about instant peace and understanding?

"I brought the berries for Dad and Grandma Rainwater," she explained.

"Does this mean you've had some success?"

She could hear the sneer in his voice but ignored it. "A little success . . . and a bit of failure."

"You're being cryptic."

"You're being cruel."

"I'm being honest, Kali." Morgan slipped his hands into the pockets of his blue jeans and looked down at his feet. "It might sound blunt, but you know me. I tell it as I see it. You've wasted a lot of time on your breeding projects this past year, and personally I was maybe hoping you'd fail *just a little bit* so you could see how foolish you've been. You're an orchardist, not a researcher."

"And what about the promises I made to Dad?"

Morgan swore under his breath. "About the berries? How could you worry about that promise when you broke the most important vow of all?"

"Morgan—we're standing less than twenty feet from Dad!"

"Dad's *grave*, Kali. You promised him you wouldn't sell the view property, and not only did you sell it, you sold it to a freakin' wind smurf. You sold your heritage. That land's been in our family for—"

"Dammit, I was put on the spot." Kali stepped back, purposefully widening the distance between her and her father's grave site even more. "I couldn't keep the land and continue the research. I-I was forced to break one promise in order to keep another! He expected more from me than he did from you."

Kali instantly regretted her words. Morgan looked as though he'd been struck a physical blow.

"High expectations, huh? If you feel that way, then why don't you give some thought to the way you've been carrying on with Quinn Sullivan? How can you be serious about a man whose life revolves around overgrown kites and ice cream, a man who plans to live here only half of the year?"

"You're so bullheaded, Morgan. Can't you see how happy I am? For once in my life, I feel . . ." Kali took a deep breath and turned away.

How could she put all her newly experienced sensations into words that Morgan would understand? The quicksilver warmth that invaded her body when Quinn entered a room or spoke her name. The tremble of anticipation when he lifted her chin with the gentle touch of a fingertip and bent to kiss her.

It wasn't just feelings and sensations. She had changed in a dozen subtle ways. Like the fruit she nurtured in her orchards, Quinn's presence had opened her eyes to so many new possibilities. What word would help Morgan understand the transformation in her? What word other than *love*? But it was too soon, too frightening to say she loved Quinn Sullivan, to even admit it in her private thoughts.

Loving Quinn, a man whose life had been shaped by
his wanderlust, could be as foolish as trying to race the
wind that blew along the ridge. And yet, she yearned
to believe that her love might be powerful enough to
tame his desire to wander.

She turned back to face her brother. His expectant
gaze made her search for words, any words that might
appease him.

"I've never felt so fulfilled, Morgan."

"Fulfilled? I think you mean distracted. There are
rumors floating around." Morgan's overprotective
streak was running in high gear. "You've had to hire
extra crew, and I heard you bungled orders for your
last spraying and, well, I won't go into detail. You're
starting to make mistakes, little sister, errors in judg-
ment."

"You have no right." Kali set the small baskets of
strawberries down on the grass. Her hands were shaking as she straightened.

"It's my right, Kali, and my *responsibility*—"
kicking at a small rock with the toe of his boot, Morgan put extra emphasis on the last word "—to be
honest with you. Your first mistake was getting involved with a boardhead."

"This is getting too deep for me, Morgan, but I
know why we're not limiting this discussion to strawberries. You're not the expert on that subject."

"And you're no expert on men. You need a man
who isn't afraid of work, a man who might be able to
give an extra hand during harvest rather than tasting
ice cream or risking his neck on the fool river."

"Where do you get off telling me what I need" Kali dropped to the grass, crossed her arms over her knees, and cradled her head. "All these years, you've frowned on anyone who came near me and threatened my work schedule. You care more about the orchards than you do about me."

"Kali—"

"I'll tell you something. I need a man who isn't afraid to have fun, Morgan. Someone who encourages me to find the child within myself and..." She hesitated to share the imagery she used to visualize the release she'd experienced. "And to let that child dance in the wind again."

"This is crazy! You're going to get into boardsailing too?"

Kali paused, open-mouthed at her brother's assumption. She laid back on her elbows on the grassy knoll and laughed. "You take things so literally, Morgan. I'm talking about allowing free time for something other than work. I'm talking about going easy on myself, letting go of guilt. And if there's one thing I've learned from this silly argument we're having, it's that I haven't really begun to put any of that in practice."

"You're not making sense."

"Neither are you. You're telling me how to live my life. You're pushing the same work ethic that Dad did, the same way of life that put him in that grave thirty years sooner than he expected."

Sister and brother stared in quiet reflection at the grave. A faint breeze rustled through the leaves of the old oak tree.

"Lord, I'm sorry, Kali," Morgan murmured as he sat down on the grassy slope beside her. "You came up here to spend time with Dad and—"

"I can spend time with Dad anytime I want to. Every time I see you, Morgan, I can't help thinking about the resemblance between you two. But as far as what Dad thinks about the way I've managed my life, that can't be so important anymore. I need to give myself approval. I need to feel it's okay to make mistakes."

"You're kidding yourself. For six years you've put all your energy into breeding your bloody berries, and suddenly you act like your research doesn't matter to you. And suddenly Dad's opinion doesn't matter to you."

"I just told you why."

"I find it hard to believe Quinn Sullivan has changed your life that much. Six months ago, you wouldn't be bringing your failed strawberries up here as a peace offering to Dad."

"Morgan, I swear you only want to hear the bad news when it comes to everything that's going on in my life. I *told* you I had a minor success, excuse me— a *major* success—with my work on Grandma's extra-sweet berries." Briefly Kali explained the hope she had for marketing the Rainwater Red strawberry as a source of natural sweetener.

While he seemed to digest this news, Morgan stared at her intently. "Damn," he swore softly. "You really were doing some work in there all this time."

"What did you think I was doing?"

"Justifying the time you spent at college while I stayed home."

"You stayed home? Morgan, you and Katy got married right out of high school and Travis was born a year later. You've been jealous of my freedom all this time. Why don't you just drop it? We're even now. We don't have to be slaves to the past and all that sibling rivalry. Why can't you let it go and learn to accept the fact that I'm a responsible and capable adult who's chosen to become involved in a relationship with an equally responsible *male* adult?"

"Responsible?" Morgan stood up and faced her. "I've caught Travis hanging around Quinn Sullivan's ice cream plant half a dozen times. Says he's looking for a summer job. Get this. My son doesn't want to help his father out this summer. He'd rather get a job with a *wind clause* that allows him a flexible schedule in case wind conditions are good for boardsailing."

"I know, Morgan. I talked to Travis—"

"He doesn't even know how to boardsail, Kali."

"Then what are you really afraid of?"

Frowning, her brother smoothed his large callused fingers against his forehead and stretched. After several moments of silence he faced her again.

"I could lose him Kali. Travis is impressionable. And right now he's not too impressed with orchard work...or his Dad. He looks at Quinn like some kind of hero. Suddenly I'm the small-town boy who never had a fancy education. I keep hearing about Quinn, how Quinn studied at Harvard and how Quinn has traveled the world."

"I'm sorry, Morgan. Try to understand what Travis is feeling. He's fifteen and it's natural to—"

"No, Kali. I'm sorry. He's all I have. Are you so blind you can't see that you're falling in love with a man who's turning my son against me?"

Quinn walked past two carpenters putting the finishing touches on the kitchen cabinets. He leaned over a counter to make notes related to the progress. Sunshine streamed through the skylight overhead, illuminating the work scene in the partially completed kitchen. The swirling eddies of sawdust captured errant sunbeams giving the entire room a feeling of distorted reality.

Between construction on his home and construction on the Queensland Ice plant, Quinn's life felt equally distorted. The only constant was Kali. She had found time when there was none by asking him to help her with some of the chores. And he'd been happy to oblige, even on those days where he'd spent twelve hours at the plant. Working alongside Kali made the most miserable of tasks far more bearable, and he was happy to offer her the gift of his time and effort.

And when the chores were done, he offered her the gift of himself. For the past week, they'd taken to sharing her four-poster bed every night. The motor home that remained in place to serve as Quinn's temporary home had become little more than a place that offered him respite from construction, and time away from Kali when the emotional pull became too intense.

"Quinn!"

He turned to find Kali on the back steps, knocking on an imaginary door.

"Come in," he laughed. "The door's wide open. Be sure to wipe your feet."

"I can't stay more than a minute," she warned, closing the phantom door behind her. "My mother just called. She's on her way."

"From Portland?"

"She called from downtown Hood River. She suddenly had an urge to see the old place and hopped in the car. Mom wants to check the progress on your house and she's excited about seeing that *wonderful young man* again."

Quinn had met Rebecca Rainwater only twice. She was impulsive, brash, opinionated, good-natured and refreshing. And she made no secret of the fact that she wanted Kali to sell the orchards to Morgan and to find a stable job and an honest man. Quinn had the feeling *he* was that man.

"Bring her over. I'll order takeout."

"Mom beat you to it. She's bringing us the lunch pastries she told you about. Chinese dim sum. I'll save a couple of barbecued pork buns for you."

"I'm not invited?" Quinn had to shout over the drills and saws being used by the carpenters. "Let's go outside to talk," he suggested, taking Kali's elbow.

"You're invited, Quinn, but I'm going to tell her you're too busy. If you come over, my mother will spend the entire visit asking you questions about your income and stability, and I want a chance to tell her about the Rainwater Red berry."

"I'll try to give you equal time," Quinn teased as he began a slow walk around the construction site. "I can't help it if your mother thinks I'm wonderful."

"Her daughter is about to change her opinion of Quinn Sullivan if you insist on joining us for lunch."

"Impossible. The opinion runs in the family—"

"With the exception of my brother."

Her easy relaxed movements became more self-conscious as she picked up a piece of splintered wood and ran her finger along the length of it.

Quinn couldn't help but observe the change in Kali. The teasing ended there. "Don't tell me. Is Morgan invited to lunch? Is that why you don't want me there?"

"I'd tell you straight out if that was the truth. I had a confrontation with Morgan two days ago at the cemetery. He seems to think you're a bad influence on Travis. He didn't make demands, but I think it'd be a bad idea to hire my nephew when you start hiring this summer."

"Too late."

"What do you mean?"

"We talked, and I promised him a job, Kali. It's June and I'm not really hiring until July, but he said he'd turn sixteen any day."

"That's true."

"And he told me his Dad didn't care one way or the other."

"Morgan cares. He wants Travis to work with him, Quinn. It's important for a kid who grows up on an orchard to learn how his family does things." Kali stopped and stared at the front of the structure. "We have traditions. I remember how my Dad told me stories about other relatives while we worked. It's part of the continuity. Maybe I couldn't feel accepted by the family until I'd paid some dues."

"You know about my past, Kali," Quinn dug his hands deeper into his pockets. "I was expected to follow in the proverbial footsteps as well. Look where it got me. The boss's son who wasn't supposed to express his ideas about a new line of natural ice cream. Morgan's a lot like my Dad. Inflexible. It might be good for Travis to work at the plant now and then."

"And where do you expect him to live?" Kali's voice was heavy with sarcasm.

"I think you're overreacting." Quinn squinted into the sun to face her. "Morgan isn't going to throw his son out of the house over a simple matter like a part-time job. What's wrong with you, Kali? I was just thinking that Travis could do both—help his Dad and earn some money for boardsailing gear by working for me."

"Boardsailing gear? Don't interfere with Morgan's parenting, Quinn. Do you understand? *Some things are sacred.*" She said each word slowly to add emphasis.

"I respect his rights as a father, but that doesn't mean he knows how to communicate with Travis effectively."

"And you've had a lot of experience in fathering?" Kali paused before a pile of broken brick.

"I know how to listen to your nephew, Kali. I try to make him feel he can be himself around me. There's no need to try to impress me."

"Maybe you like the hero worship." She edged her toe against the small pile of brick. It toppled slowly. "You could actually be more harmful to Travis than helpful."

One of the workmen sauntered out to his truck and looked in their direction. The construction noise had stopped. Great, Quinn thought. He and Kali were raising their voices before a lunchtime crowd.

"Kali," Quinn softened his tone and began walking toward her house. "I'm not trying to take over Morgan's position as father. It's just that I can really relate to Travis. When I was a kid in California, my heroes carried surf boards. My father carried a briefcase, complained about the hard work and didn't have time for me."

"I suppose there's a strong bond there," she agreed. "Which is strange, because I have a strong bond with Travis as well." She told Quinn about the afternoon she'd spent with the boy. "Maybe I'm jealous of the effect you have on him. I want to be the person to rescue him from a future he doesn't want."

Quinn noted they were standing halfway between their homes. "I've hurt your feelings, haven't I?"

"A little. It's just an issue that no one can solve at the moment. The only thing I'm asking you to do is to avoid hiring Travis."

"I'm sorry, Kali." He'd lost patience, not with her, but with the issue. There was no way out except to stand his ground. "I made Travis a promise and I'll keep it. If you'll excuse me."

"Quinn—"

"Enough!" He held up a hand as though to stop the flow of words. "I'm heading to the plant for the afternoon. Save me those barbecued pork buns, okay?"

"The news about your strawberry is very interesting, Kali, but let's be serious. It's going to take years to benefit from it." Using her chopsticks expertly, Rebecca Rainwater picked up a piece of parchment chicken and dipped it in soy sauce. "I still can't believe you told Quinn you wanted to eat with me in private. Look at all this food."

"Mom, could you stop talking about Quinn Sullivan for a minute." Kali decided to try a diplomatic approach. Her mother was basically good-natured, and their relationship had always been one of relaxed camaraderie with occasional sparring.

"He's the best thing that's ever happened to you, honey. Hmm, try this one with hot mustard."

"I disagree. The best thing that's ever happened to me was the way I've *chosen* to approach my relationship with Quinn."

"How's that?"

"With cautious optimism. More tea?"

"Uh-huh. I could use a warm-up. I wish you would stop being so cautious." The older woman gave Kali an exasperated smile. "The man is financially secure, confident, worldly, gorgeous—go ahead and have another potsticker, you're still too thin—and it's obvious he cares about you. I like his style, I like his taste and he's athletic, which means he'll live a long time. Longer than your father."

Kali felt a pang for her mother, who had grieved stoically for six months before moving to Portland to live with Kali's aunt. She bitterly blamed the orchards for her husband's early death.

"Now tell me what you're leading up to, Mother, or do I really have to ask?"

"It's simple. I approve of Quinn. You have my blessing. I know you're not asking for one, but he's perfect for you. Think of it, summer's just starting. Thousands of beautiful young women will be following the wind to Hood River, and if you were smart you'd straighten out your life now."

"Straighten out my life? You make it sound like a snarled piece of yarn."

"Why not sell your land to Morgan and take on a teaching job here in town?"

"I still have the strawberries, Mom."

"They're a gamble. But then, most things in life are a gamble. I should know. I loved your father, but I was starry-eyed when we took over the orchards. Gave up my teaching career to help Harlan and, well, you know the rest of the story."

"You loved the work, Mom. I remember the way it was. Especially at harvesttime. No challenge was too big for us back then and—"

"I think you're romanticizing the past, Kali. We had some pretty hard times. The Rainwater household bore no resemblance to *Little House on the Prairie*. If you want a stable future, you'll give your relationship with Quinn more serious thought."

Kali held back a choking laugh. "Honestly, Mom. You're beginning to sound like a matchmaker from the old country. I appreciate the advice but—"

"It makes sense, you know. I'm sure you realize it's one way to get the view property back in the family."

Inhaling deeply, Kali took a sip of Oolong tea from her cup. During the past few days she'd had confrontations with Morgan and Quinn. Was her mother going to join the pack?

She saw the older woman as a friend in many ways. Though Rebecca Rainwater's lack of interest in her strawberry breeding project annoyed her at times, she knew it was rooted in maternal fear.

"I'm more than a bit offended by your suggestion that I might profit through marriage, Mom. I've spent a lot of time examining my feelings and looking for any sign that my love for the land is wrapped up in any way with my interest in Quinn."

"I didn't mean to offend you, honey. I just want to see you secure and happy and married. You'd make a wonderful mother with all your nurturing qualities. Why waste that on plants?"

"Mother, please." Kali just shook her head. "Let me handle my feelings for Quinn my way."

"No. I know you too well. You'll sit through four seasons thinking about those feelings. You're so tied to the land, Kali. You'll want to know whether Quinn knows how to snuggle properly during those long winter months."

"Nice thought, but he won't be here. He's a half-a-year man." Kali began setting aside the barbecued pork buns to take to him. "Quinn will never spend a real winter with me. He'll be enjoying Australia's summer at that time, then he'll head back up here every year and enjoy another long season of sun."

"But you'd be willing to follow him, wouldn't you?"

"Down under?" Kali held the warm teacup between her palms. "Mother, I haven't the faintest idea."

Eight

Glancing out his tinted office window, Quinn spotted Kali's truck pulling up in the parking lot of Queensland Ice headquarters. When she climbed out of the cab of the pickup, she was carrying a pink cardboard box, immediately identifying the contents as Chinese takeout.

Quinn was touched that she'd remembered his barbecue pork buns, but was she still angry about their discussion over Travis working for him? He watched her head toward the partially completed building with determined strides. The wind lifted the skirt of her sundress exposing an enticing stretch of thigh. While he watched her battle the relentless wind, a plan formed slowly in his mind.

Glancing at his desktop, Quinn grabbed a hat from

the samples left by the design company and hurried to the building's entrance.

Kali gave him a cool glance as she stepped around a pile of construction debris.

"Excuse me, Ms. Rainwater, do you enjoy ice cream?"

"Quinn, I don't have time to play games. I brought your pork buns because I felt sorry for you, losing that argument with me and all." She pressed the pink box against his stomach. "I hope you don't choke on your lunch. Enjoy."

"Not so fast, Kali." Quinn stepped back when she pressed the box a second time. He slipped the clerk's hat with the Queensland Ice logo onto his head. "Why don't we forget our misunderstanding about Travis for now. I desperately need your help."

"What kind of help, and just how desperate are you?" She frowned.

"Remember how I tasted your strawberries for you?"

"That wasn't official. You just ate them."

"Well, this is just a little bit more official, but it's something we can do together. Seriously, Kali, are you up for tasting a new flavor?"

"Quinn, don't be ridiculous. I'm sure you have a professional tester of some kind hired for your plant."

"*I'm* the taste tester."

"Well, you're not even in full production yet. You haven't finished the building or hired all the innocent sons away from their hardworking fathers."

"I'm not going to respond to that barb. I'm trying to put this morning's misunderstandings aside, and there's another reason for asking you to sample my test batches. I'm rather proud of our product, Grasshopper.''

"It's a deal. You know I love ice cream. You eat the cold pork buns and I'll give your new flavor a try.''

"That's the name of the flavor? St. Uhro's Ice?'' Kali adjusted her blindfold and remained seated on the soft cushioned sofa Quinn had led her to, waiting for further instruction. "Is that a take-off on *St. Elmo's Fire*, Mr. Sullivan?''

"Coincidence. Pure coincidence.'' Quinn's was the voice of innocence.

"Then it's mint flavored, right? As in the grasshoppers they serve after the St. Uhro Day parade here in Hood River?''

"I'm not going to ruin the surprise, Kali. Just taste it.'' She felt Quinn press the handle of a spoon into her right palm. He guided her left hand to a cold dish in front of her, on what appeared to be a coffee table. "Now clear your mind of any expectations,'' he added.

"I can expect it to be good.''

"It's very good. Stop waving the spoon around and stick it in the test batch.''

Kali intentionally gave the spoon an extra wave before she lowered it into the mound of hard ice cream. "Firmly packed, I'd say.''

"I *know* how it's packed. I want to know how it *tastes*.''

"Somehow you seem bossier when I'm blind-folded, Quinn.''

"Kali—"

"I'm tasting, I'm tasting." Trying to avoid a near miss, she lifted the spoon to her mouth cautiously. "It's so cold it almost burns. This isn't dry ice, is it?"

"T-a-s-t-e."

Kali let the small spoonful of ice cream sit on her tongue. "It's more chocolate than mint . . . and full of hmm—crunchy things," she concluded.

"Do the crunchy things distract you from the flavor?"

"Distract? If I could see them—" she reached for the blindfold but he stopped her "—I'd feel a whole lot better. All I can picture are all the grasshopper costumes marching in the annual parade. You didn't hunt up a handful of hoppers for your St. Uhro's Ice, did you?"

"First you accuse me of feeding you dry ice, now it's raw grasshoppers."

"Meaning you've cooked them?"

"Kali . . ."

"I like it, really. I like chocolate and I like mint and I like having my ice cream filled with lots of chunks of chocolate and nuts or whatever, but these are pretty crispy little things."

"Do they leave an aftertaste?"

"What do you expect—tobacco?"

"Kali, I didn't put grasshoppers in the test batch. Why don't you give me your overall opinion. Would you call it creamy or super creamy?"

She blindly took another spoonful. "Super creamy."

"Chunky or extra chunky?"

"It's extra everything, Quinn. It's super creamy, super chunky, super flavorful, super wonderful. In fact, I'd like a little more."

"We made a very small test batch today, but I have another flavor here I'd like you to try." There was a husky rasp to Quinn's voice, a change of tone that alerted Kali to the importance of the next flavor. "I tried more than one of your strawberries that night in the greenhouse, so it's only fair that you help me as much as you can with my experiment."

"I'm willing to try it—" She barely got the words out before she felt the firm contour of Quinn's mouth press against her half-parted lips. She moaned against the shock of expecting cold and receiving the sudden warmth of his searching tongue.

The kiss began deep and desperate with need before gentling into a slow swirling exploration along the inner edge of her teeth and the soft hidden recesses of her mouth.

The blindfold offered her a heightened awareness of the movements of his mouth. "Quinn!" she gasped against the onslaught of pleasure. "Aren't we in some kind of testing area?"

Quinn chuckled as he slipped the blindfold up. "We're somewhere dark—" his fingers skimmed down her throat to the V neckline of her sundress "—and intimate." He captured her moan with his mouth. "Welcome to my office, Ms. Rainwater."

Despite the subdued lighting, she was aware of bold colors and smooth contours. It was as though Quinn had taken the freedom, fluidity and vibrant tones associated with boardsailing and incorporated them all into his personal space. He settled on the sofa beside her.

"I'm impressed," she whispered.

"With my office or with my skills?"

"I'll just say I'm impressed with the skills you're displaying in your office. We've spent a lot of time in my four-poster bed. I get the feeling we're in your territory now."

"Welcome to my world, Grasshopper. I am feeling a bit territorial." His fingers caught in her hair. He pressed his forehead to hers and paused. She heard his sharp intake of breath. "Don't move. I'm going to try to forget I'm at work."

Quinn moved quickly to a nearby console. Within seconds the subdued lighting was dimmed further. The clear sweet melody of a flute filled the room, soon followed by other wind instruments. The music and dark intimacy altered the perimeters of the room for Kali. She felt a heavy tremble of anticipation.

"What about your employees?"

"There's a great wind blowing, so those employees I do have are out on the water taking advantage of their wind clauses."

"Are you trying to tell me that we have the place to ourselves?"

"I was trying to be subtle."

"Forget about subtle, Quinn." She initiated the kiss this time, molding her lips to his as she moved her fingers up the hollows of his throat to trace his firm jawline.

Firm or stubborn? Her hand paused as she recalled the heated discussion of that morning. Then quickly she dismissed all thoughts of their conflict. Taking his lower lip gently between her teeth, she drew lazy patterns back and forth with her tongue until he moaned her name.

"You're wonderful, Kali." His words reverberated against her lips and she smiled in response.

Releasing his mouth, she began gliding her tongue along the edge of his jaw. She felt the warmth of one of his fingers stroking the hollow between her breasts.

Kali pulled back slightly enjoying the vision of Quinn's dark good looks, and the way a shock of his hair had fallen over his forehead. His eyes had darkened with desire. She felt caressed by their inner warmth.

She smiled as she focused on his mouth, the firm sculpted lips and even teeth, that same gentle knowing smile that formed on his lips whenever they lay together in the lamplight of her room.

There was something breathlessly exciting and forbidden about their being together in this room, in near darkness. Without direct light or shadow, there seemed a clarity of thought and sensation. Kali felt her desire for Quinn rapidly escalating.

Then his finger brushed against her lower lip and she leaned back and parted her mouth in response. She smiled as the stroking continued, and Quinn carried the movement to each corner of her mouth.

"Relax, Grasshopper. Don't think about anything or anyone but yourself. Enjoy the feelings."

Exhaling, she felt her limbs relax and grow warm. He began a languid stroking of her legs, his hand moving beneath the sundress to caress her inner thighs.

Kali found herself moving to the rhythm of his hands, to his whispered words of encouragement.

Each journey of his hand became bolder. His fingers grazed then edged inside the narrow band of lace between her legs and found her softness unerringly. She moaned against the pleasurable sensations his hand brought.

Gently he lowered her head to the sofa cushions. Her long silken hair moved like water over his arm, and he gloried in the sensation. When she reached out and touched the buckle of his belt, he lifted her hand and kissed her fingertips.

"No, sweet," he whispered. "Allow me."

Watching her eyes widen as he slipped out of his slacks and shrugged out of his shirt made his waiting all the more unbearable.

He slid his hands over the smooth satin sweep of her thighs. With deliberate tenderness, he pulled the dainty lace panties from her legs. He spread her thighs and entered her one exquisite inch at a time. She moaned his name and reached out to him blindly. Her fingers touched his shoulders, and he felt the bite of her nails as he penetrated her further.

"Yes, yes." She moaned. The dim lighting left so much to the imagination but nothing more was needed. Quinn was making her feel complete.

In matched rhythms they climbed the crest of rapture. There was no gentleness to their loving, only the intense driving need fed by unbridled passion, a need that took them past all thought and reason to the clouds beyond.

Quinn collapsed beside her on the large sofa, pulling her body close as their passion flowed into contentment.

Still trembling, Kali found a focus in Quinn's roguish smile.

"Our interview seems to have been interrupted, Mr. Sullivan. Do you want me to continue my evaluation?"

"Hmmm, I'd love it," he murmured.

"All right." She ran a finger over the bridge of his nose. "I'll give you high marks for smoothness. You were very smooth."

"Thank you."

"Your packaging was attractive as always. Especially your eyes. I should have known you'd cooked up something special."

"Professionalism, please."

Nine

Stupid wind! Stupid river!'' Kali emerged sputtering from a record-breaking twenty splashdowns within a ten minute period then reached out and hit the sailboard forcefully with her hand. "Stupid board!"

"Easy on the equipment." Quinn sighed with silent exasperation as Kali positioned herself in the waist-high water to attempt another water start. "Give it a rest. I told you before we left the farm that I didn't expect you to turn into a master boardsailer in one day. You've done great with everything else. Believe me when I say water starts take time and practice."

"But I studied the book and—"

"Get into the support position!" Quinn yelled. "Foot on the board—quick, on the board!"

"—and I practiced it on dry land *all morning*!"

"Chest to the knee—front arm straight!"

"I know that!"

Quinn grimaced as Kali was blown sideways several feet and deposited in one unglorious splash in the river. "Then why don't you do it, know-it-all," he muttered to himself. "I've never met such a stubborn neophyte." When she surfaced, he smiled weakly and gave a halfhearted wave. "Another brave try."

"Bull!" Kali's curse-the-wind, curse-the-board, curse-the-water, hit-the-board-hard routine started over again.

Quinn harbored thoughts of holding Kali underwater momentarily. Had she sent her evil twin to try his patience?

Her hostility had surfaced two days earlier when he'd begun going over the safety aspects of the sport. That morning he'd taught Kali how to rig with his teeth clenched much of the time. The self-rescue lesson involved alternating biting and holding his tongue.

And this from an athletic woman who'd excelled in every attempt—until the waterstart.

"You're trying too hard. Come on, we're taking a break." No longer attempting to conceal his frustration, Quinn swore under his breath. "Stop being such a perfectionist. Why don't you give yourself permission to make mistakes, to be a beginner?"

"Quinn, I've lived here all my life! This is *my* river and I should be able to do this!"

"Great logic. Should all Californians who live in coastal areas know how to surf?"

"They should know more about surfing than people who stroll in from all over the world."

"Nonsense. Beach your craft and take a breather, Kali. I think you've got too much water in your ears."

"This is my hometown, Quinn. People will recognize me. I have my pride, you know. I won't leave here today until I do a perfect water start."

When she began to move into the support position, Quinn took command of her rented sailboard. "That does it. Give it a rest, Rainwater. Concentrate on the positive. You did a fair job of sailing across and turning. I was impressed. You did pretty good for a beginner. Native of Hood River or not."

"Pretty good isn't good enough for me."

Quinn began pulling her board and sail toward the beach. He'd chosen the south shore of The Hook because it was protected from Westerlies by Wells Island and because of the crowds, figuring Kali would feel less self-conscious in the company of other beginners. The plan had backfired. She seemed to feel everyone recognized her as a native of the area. He had to get her mind off the townspeople and focused on viewing boardsailing as a nondestructive way of dealing with Mother Nature.

"I think I understand your problem, Kali."

"Then why didn't you tell me about my problem when I was out there struggling with my water start?"

After looking around for nosy spectators and finding none, Quinn released her board from his grasp. It floated on the water between them creating a colorful barrier as he confronted his pupil. "Why did you ask me to teach you in the first place?"

"Because—" she stammered, pushing dripping strands of her long hair back from her face "—I don't know. Maybe I simply wanted to know why you love it so much.''

"You could have asked me why I love boardsailing, Kali," he said, softening his tone one decibel.

"But I wanted more than that. I wanted to *feel* why. Experience it firsthand . . . like you've experienced the work I do in my orchards."

"I appreciate what you're saying, but you're a bit of a handful in the water."

"What's that supposed to mean?"

"Not only are you fighting my efforts to teach you, you're fighting the wind and the water and your natural instincts."

"My natural instincts are not telling me how to water start." She put both palms on the sailboard that rested between them on the water.

"I'm talking about going with the flow, listening to your inner voice, feeling the force and *Chi'* of your body and becoming one with nature."

Kali looked around at the other boardsailors in the water, then glanced back at Quinn. "Are you serious? I don't hear any of the other instructors around here talking about the force."

"You're hearing *me*. Because I feel it's essential to the way you approach the sport."

"I just want to be able to get up on the board and stay there long enough to show off this wet suit we rented for the day."

"Kali, let me assure you—you look great in and out of the water, and I'll go into more detail about that tonight when we're alone." Quinn cleared his throat. "But your appearance isn't the issue right now."

"No speeches, please. I had a thousand chores I could have done today, but I wanted to come down here and experience this. Please—just teach me to boardsail."

Her expression was suddenly wistful, her voice pleading, and Quinn felt his heart performing an erratic slalom within his chest cavity.

"I plan to teach you more as soon as you decide to listen—and commit yourself to learning to understand the forces of nature, the wind and water—"

"You're going to stand here in waist-deep water and explain nature to me? Hah! I've spent my entire life fighting the forces of nature. I've been a slave to the weather!" Kali gave the sailboard a shove. It sloshed toward Quinn but the current slapped it back to Kali. She gave it an incredulous look.

"Let me tell you about the wind," she continued. "Have you ever bought five hundred dollars worth of chemicals, had the equipment out in the field to spray and had a wind come up—the kind of 'nuclear wind' you boardsailors dream about—and suddenly the orchardist finds herself throwing a five hundred dollar investment to the wind—literally pissing in the wind?"

"Kali—"

"Then there's drought and frost and heavy rains, thunder and lightning, hail, snow, ice storms, locusts, floods and acts of God."

"Acts of God?"

"Well—"

"I think you've made your point. More than made your point. It appears you've struggled with nature all your life, Kali."

"You bet I have."

"And have you won yet?"

"What do you mean?"

"Have you ever wondered what it would be like to become one with the wind, to harness those forces and renew your own energy as a result?"

"I can only imagine," she said quietly as she moved her hand through the water that lapped at her hips.

"Maybe it's a bit like making love," he tried putting the feeling into words. "When two people unite in harmony they create a new energy, in a sense they become one."

"Try to understand. I've always seen the wind as a force that has the potential to disrupt my work, in a sense, destroy my world."

"Sometimes I can't help wondering if you choose to look at relationships in the same way, Kali." Quinn left the words hanging between them for a moment. "With the potential to destroy your world."

"I'm not sure if that's fair. I've opened up a lot with you, Quinn."

"But you're still fighting your feelings, aren't you? Being cautious can sometimes complicate things. There are issues between us that need airing. I want to clear things up, and you want to gloss over them."

"I feel overloaded. When you're not confronting me, I'm being confronted by Morgan, Travis or my mother." She laughed and shook her head. "I'll have to ask people to start taking numbers when they enter the house if this keeps up."

Quinn appreciated Kali's attempt at humor, but he couldn't ignore his own feelings. She'd hurt him.

"All I want now is a part of your trust, Kali. It would strengthen our relationship, and it certainly can't hurt the way you're approaching this boardsailing lesson."

"I'm sorry if you can't understand why I am the way I am, Quinn." Frowning, she looked down at the sailboard floating in front of her and ran her palm back and forth over its slick surface. "I'm earthbound. Rooted firmly here in Hood River and feeling those roots shake every time I look out on the water and see an armada of boardsailors. You and people like you threaten to change my way of life, change my sleepy little town—"

"Wake up, Kali. There's nothing sleepy about your town. And it's not just the so-called wind smurfs," he chided. "I'm a businessman. I checked into the economics of this area before selecting Hood River as a site for our North American plant. I know there have been hard times, and I know that some people see the boardsailors as an economic boom for the valley, but it's you—the orchardists and the lumber industry— that keep this paradise thriving."

"It's not a matter of economics. Our life-style's being changed."

"Try opening your mind to change, Kali. We aren't a threat to you. Now you have me doing it—this me-and-you-and-we-business, as if we're choosing up sides. It's ridiculous."

"That's easy for you to say. You don't stand to lose as much as I do."

"You're not going to lose anything, Kali. Is that why you're resisting the sailboard, resisting my lessons? Do you see all this as enemy territory?" he asked with a forced chuckle. "Do you see me as a threat to you?"

"Maybe."

"I admire so many things about you. The way you tend living things, your ties to the past, your deep roots. I wouldn't want you to turn your back on your heritage to please me. That's why it's important to talk about these things. Now is there anything I can do to make you feel differently about our lessons?"

"Just be patient and help me with my water start. I'm determined to get it right."

With some effort, Kali began positioning her board and sail, refusing his assistance at one point.

"And there's something else you can do," she added moments later. "Tell me how to become one with nature...starting with those lips of yours." Supporting her weight with her palms, Kali leaned over the board, and offered him a kiss.

"You're as stubborn as I am," Quinn said with a sigh. "All right, back into the support position!"

"Looking for something for your wahine?" the female clerk asked Quinn. "We've got that suit in hot pink, bright turquoise, jade, and flaming red. It's a big seller. Any particular size?"

"Thanks for asking, but I'm just looking right now," he replied with a smile, stepping back from the rack.

Five young boardheads walked by, their tanned bodies garbed in tropical prints, their faces displaying the same pattern of Day-Glow zinc oxide war paint. He couldn't decide what was more colorful—the wet suits and bikinis he'd been looking at in the surf shop or the customers.

No matter. He found it hard to resist buying every suit in the store for Kali. He'd been glowing with pride for two days.

She'd perfected her water start during their first lesson. The lesson lasted ten hours and left both of them emotionally and physically drained, but Kali was learning to harness the forces of wind and water, to become one with nature.

He wanted to surprise her with a sleek new swimsuit to celebrate her successful effort. Then she'd need a wet suit and eventually her own boards, sails, masts, boom sets, universal joint unit, a harness and of course a dry suit for those cold water days.

His desire to outfit her completely was getting ahead of reality. Chances were Kali would take a few lessons, learn the basics, progress well because of her natural ability, and because of her limited time, enjoy the sport for occasional leisure only. After all his speeches about not wanting her to turn her back on her heritage, he didn't want her to feel pressure to leave her work in the orchards and meet him daily on the shores of the Columbia.

He just wanted her to know how special she was.

His hand strayed to the iridescent purple suit, cut high on the hip, low in the neckline. It was easy to envision the daring design stretching provocatively across her tall slender body.

He was holding the suit up for inspection when he felt a tap on his shoulder.

"Hey dude, whatcha' doin' in here?" a male voice announced from behind.

Turning, Quinn found Travis smiling sheepishly. The boy was wearing wild surf trunks, deck shoes, and a logo T-shirt and was sporting an exaggerated devil-may-care attitude.

"Hey, Travis. I'm ah, just doing a little shopping."

"For Aunt Kali?"

"She mentioned something the other day about needing a new swimsuit, so I thought I'd surprise her."

"Yeah, but she doesn't go to the beach. I don't think she'd get much use out of it. I doubt if she's even got tan lines or anything."

"She doesn't," Quinn answered before realizing the implication of his remark. "That is . . . she intends to spend more time on her tan this year."

"Chill out, man," Travis spoke in a quiet aside. "I've heard my Dad talking about the two of you. It's cool. I don't have a problem with you guys sleeping together or nothin'."

"You don't?" Quinn felt a ripple of irritation. "Don't get the wrong idea. We haven't been overly worried about your approval. What we do in private is our business, you understand that, don't you?"

"Sure. I just figured it was happening because you spend so much time with Aunt Kali and stuff. I wasn't trying to talk to you about it or nothin'. Man, I'm not stupid. That kind of stuff is private.''

''I took Kali to The Hook a couple of days ago for her first boardsailing lesson.''

''Really? Gosh, I wish I could have been there. How did she do?''

''Terrific. She's a natural athlete, and the orchard work keeps her fit. A little stubborn when it comes to some things, but I'm proud of her, Travis. You should feel the same way about her. And about your Dad as well.''

''Yeah, I guess I should.'' The teenager looked crestfallen.

''Something bothering you?'' Quinn put the swimsuit back on the rack and turned his full attention to Travis.

''Not really. I don't know. Well, I guess I'm wondering about a couple of things, but I'm not sure if I should ask.''

''I can't say anything until I know what you're talking about.'' The speakers overhead were blaring pulsating music. ''Why don't we step outside where I can hear you?''

Travis followed Quinn to the sidewalk. The boy leaned against the garish exterior of the building. ''Out of any of the boardsailors, I bet you'd be the best teacher. I really wanna learn now before summer gets going.''

''I'd be happy to teach you, Travis. Kali rented all her gear, but I'm sure I've got some old equipment I can put together for you sometime. How does your Dad feel about all this?''

"Man, I don't know. He's still steamed about a bunch of other stuff."

"And you think taking boardsailing lessons is going to improve your relationship?"

"It can't get worse. I gotta ask you something else. You must think I'm goin' to pester you all the time."

"No, I don't. What is it?"

"It's about the summer job you promised me, the one at Queensland Ice?"

"Uh-huh."

"I got a problem to work out with my Dad. He wants me helping him with the Bartlett pear harvest starting around early August." Travis began walking down the sidewalk as he talked, his shoulders hunched as if he carried the weight of the world. "So I may have to work a different schedule then or something."

"I'm sure we can find something flexible, Travis. I'm more concerned about how your Dad feels about you working for me at all."

Quinn glanced back at the surf shop, pondering the question of whether to buy the iridescent purple suit for Kali. When he turned to catch up with Travis, the teenager had such an intense expression on his face that Quinn knew the boy's issues were far weightier than a few ounces of purple fabric.

"You know," Quinn continued, "your father doesn't exactly approve of my life-style or my relationship with your Aunt Kali. I'm not sure if he thinks I'd be good company for you."

"It's a trip, man. He's just so old-fashioned." Travis shrugged his shoulders and dug his hands into his pockets. "The truth is, sometimes my Dad can act like a real jerk."

"Compared to the way you think he should act?"

"Compared to the way you'd act."

A wave of guilt washed over Quinn. "What makes you think you know how I'd act in any given situation? That's a bit presumptuous. I don't have the stress of running a farm or being a single parent raising a fifteen-year-old son."

"But you'd be cool about things, dude. You'd approve of someone my age getting a board and sail and learning the sport."

"Travis, I'm your neighbor and I have a relationship with your aunt and I might be your employer soon as well. I don't mind you calling me Quinn but please don't call me dude, okay?"

"Yeah, that's cool. See what I mean? You talk to me like an equal or almost an equal. Close anyway. My Dad can't handle me being an adult now."

"An adult?"

Travis paused to study his reflection in the shop window. "Yeah, it's tough on me. He thinks I'm some kind of kid but I'll be sixteen next week."

"I remember it well. Tough age. I had problems with my Dad when I was sixteen."

"What happened?"

"I wanted to be a surfer back then. He wanted me to study to go into business with him. He runs a food manufacturing monopoly."

"Wow, so you became a surfer then switched to boardsailing?"

"No, I went to school on the East Coast and studied to go into the family business, and whenever I came home from school, I caught some waves in California."

"But you didn't work for your father in the end, right?"

"Wrong. I worked for him for a number of years. That's how I got practical experience with ice cream production. Look, I'm not in the mood to give you my life history, Travis. I just want you to know you're not the first sixteen-year-old kid to have problems with his father. But the last thing I want is trouble from Morgan. Or more trouble between Morgan and Kali because of me hiring you or me teaching you how to sail."

"That's cool. So, Quinn, whatever happened to your Dad? You guys close or what?"

"I haven't seen my father for five years, Travis."

"Bummer, man. Sorry to hear it. Look, I do have a few chores at home. I should get goin', but it was good to see you. Is Kali bringing you to my birthday dinner?"

"Wouldn't miss it."

"Good. We can talk about lessons then, huh?"

"No problem, see you then." Quinn gave Travis a slap on the shoulder and watched the boy walk off.

Much of the devil-may-care attitude had worn off during their conversation. He'd caught glimpses of Travis's vulnerability and pain. The experience had brought back memories . . . and regrets that were hard to shake.

Quinn waited until Travis had turned the corner before heading back to the surf shop to buy the purple swimsuit. And while he was there, he decided, he'd check out gift possibilities for a sixteen-year-old adult.

Ten

Rebecca Rainwater led Kali, Morgan, Travis, Quinn and various assorted relatives in a rousing *Happy Birthday* song. Kali studied the candle-lit face of her nephew, swallowing hard at the sight of the tall, handsome boy preparing to blow his candles out.

Kali had been close to sixteen when his mother had died. The full-time job of bringing up Travis had become a joint family responsibility for Morgan, Kali, Rebecca and Harlan Rainwater. But Kali had been the one Travis clung to, the name he called in the night, the recipient of his childhood bouquets and clay handprints. She'd read him stories of travel and adventure, taught him to swing a bat and tie his shoes, listened to his tales of woe and bought him the special extras that brighten a child's world.

More frequently than she cared to recall, Kali had stilled Morgan's hand when it came to harsh discipline. Her brother's need to control others seemed exaggerated when it came to Travis. How many times had she looked into the child's pleading eyes and seen a reflection of her own childhood?

Now, at sixteen, Travis was as unpredictable as the gorge winds. She needed far more than a weather station to predict his ever-changing moods. She feared he'd slip out of their lives forever if Morgan didn't begin to put more effort into understanding his son's emotional needs.

"Don't forget to make a wish, honey!" Rebecca Rainwater urged her grandson. "And go ahead and be greedy when you do!"

Travis laughed, then grew silent for a moment as he appeared to reflect on the sixteen brightly burning candles. Then his eyes moved upward to his father's face and for a moment their gazes locked.

The boy glanced at Quinn then quickly looked away, inhaled deeply and turned Morgan's dining room into darkness with a single breath.

"Who wants cake?" Kali asked quickly when the lights came on. "Oh, and Quinn brought some ice cream for everyone to sample. It's called St. Uhro's Ice."

"Yuck, I'll have vanilla please!" someone quipped from the living room.

"Trust me. This ice cream was highly rated by Kali in an earlier taste test. Come on, I need guinea pigs," Quinn elaborated, "and I value your opinion—good or bad."

Kali caught the mischievous sidelong glance from Quinn. "What? You didn't bring blindfolds for all of my relatives?" she asked in a whisper.

"You were a special case. And always will be. I'll save an exclusive sample for you for later, Grasshopper."

The teasing made her feel lighthearted again. After cutting the cake, Kali made an effort to chat with an elderly aunt and paused now and then to watch Quinn socializing with her other relatives.

He had no trouble finding common ground with anyone it seemed. Warm and good-natured, he was full of empathy when needed, good humor when called for. He had a knack for making himself approachable and was drawn to the laughter of the younger children. He was content to sit alone and watch as well, his body relaxed, his features open, his contagious smile ever on the ready.

"Time to open presents!" Rebecca announced.

From her position in the dining room Kali watched Travis saunter into the living room, red-faced with embarrassment. Kali knew he disliked the family get-togethers. "It's just a chance for my Dad to talk to someone and suddenly remember old family rules and decide he'll use them on me," Travis had told her on the phone that afternoon.

Judging from the way Morgan was listening to some of the older men talk about "the way things were back then," she mused, her brother was gathering ample information for future torture.

"There's just enough fresh coffee in this pot to warm up that cup in your hand," Quinn offered from his spot beside the beverage table. "Rebecca went to make fresh if you want to wait."

"I'll take what I can get now." He took her cup and topped it off, then set it on the table. He touched her shoulder gently.

"When I was a kid, I saw families like yours at the beach or picnicking in parks—you know, a big group where everyone seemed welcomed no matter what their age—and I always thought it'd be nice to belong to those people." While he paused, he moved his hand down her upper arm and squeezed gently. "Tonight, I'm still a kid wanting to belong."

It was such a simple, honest statement. Kali experienced a sudden realization. It was important, no *essential*, for her to believe that Quinn Sullivan would fit into her extended family, that he'd feel connected to these people, especially Travis and Morgan. Why hadn't she realized before how much that meant to her? He would have to understand and respect the love she had for her family.

"Quinn." She hesitated, feeling a need to find the right words. "Have you ever tried to patch things up with your mother and father? Don't you miss seeing your sister? I mean, you've never even mentioned her name to me."

"I haven't, have I?" His voice was suddenly strained. "It's not like this, Kali." He nodded toward the living room. "People relaxed and laughing, catching up on family news, joking about someone's cooking and, well,—any of this. Now I know why you're such a loving person, Kali. It's genetic."

"But what about your mother? Doesn't she—"

"I really don't want to talk about my family, okay? I'll just borrow your relatives for the night and enjoy myself."

"Fine." Kali smiled back at Quinn. "I rent them by the hour."

"And this one's from..." Travis looked at the small tag on the large package. His features brightened and he eagerly searched around the living room. "Gosh, I didn't expect anything from you, Quinn."

"Go ahead. Open it."

Travis tore open the box and scattered the tissue paper to reveal a full wet suit. "Chill out or what. I can't believe it. I don't know how to thank you, Quinn. Now I won't look like a bumpkin on the beach when you give me those boardsailing lessons."

Aside from a few gasps from the younger children, the room had grown silent. Kali noted the older relatives focused on Morgan while the younger people focused on Quinn Sullivan. She riveted her attention on Travis.

"Why's everybody so quiet?" he asked no one in particular. "This is a really great present."

"It's real pretty with all the bright colors—the same colors those boardheads seem to like so much," a diplomatic aunt observed in a cautious tone.

"Well, I guess I'm quiet 'cuz I'm a little surprised that you'd even want to learn somethin' like that, Travis," Great-uncle Frank from Yakima intoned. "Lord knows you're busy enough helping your Dad out."

Kali felt pity for Travis, whose bubble of joy was developing a fast leak. "You probably don't know this," she announced loudly to the gathering, "but I gave it a try myself. I rented the gear, and Quinn took me out to the Hook, and I think it's a great way to look at our river from a different angle."

"Kali's good at it. I'd say she's just about ready to jibe," Quinn added.

"Jiiibbbe?" Uncle Roscoe frowned. "How would a person spell a word like that?"

"J-i-b-e," Travis complied, getting to his feet to demonstrate. "It's when you flip your sail to make a turn. First you release the boom hand and grab the mast—"

"Travis, sweetheart, why don't you sit down." Rebecca Rainwater cleared her throat forcefully and caught her grandson's full attention. "I'm not sure if your Uncle Roscoe needs to know more than the spelling of the word. It might be a good idea for you to go ahead and open the next gift. How about that blue package from Uncle Frank?"

"I haven't spoken to Travis," Morgan threw his mother a quick cutting glance. "Does a father still get a chance to talk to his son in this family?"

"Lord have mercy," Quinn whispered under his breath.

Sure that she was the only one to hear, Kali glanced over at him. He looked relaxed but she could feel tension in the hand he left resting on her shoulder.

"Travis, I'm not going to embarrass you in front of family," Morgan spoke calmly and quietly. "I'll talk to you and Quinn Sullivan later tonight. That's all I have to say.''

Kali recognized the cold even tone of her brother's voice. It was frequently followed by an emotional outburst or a day of chilling silence.

The party resumed on a less celebratory note. Uncle Roscoe told a ribald joke while Travis opened Great-uncle Frank's gift.

"I went through every room on the bottom floor and found these strays,'' Quinn announced to Kali an hour later as he carried a tray of dirty plates into the kitchen. Goodbyes had been said. Rebecca Rainwater and the other relatives had headed down the long driveway, while some remained gathered on the front walk, easing into their farewells.

"Be honest.'' He set the tray on the counter. "Do you think anyone will ever invite this gift-giving wind smurf to another birthday dinner?''

"You'll get invited back,'' Kali assured him. "Everyone loved the test batch of St. Uhro's Ice, didn't they? Of course, you'll only be welcome if you remember to bring ice cream.''

"Or if I bring you?''

"Quinn—'' Kali opened the dishwasher and began loading cups on the top rack "—I was more than a little surprised by the generosity of your gift. Why would you even consider buying a wet suit for Travis?''

"I'm impulsive. You know that. I see. I want. I buy. And I happened to be buying a gift for you at the same time. I was in a generous mood.''

"Well, I'm glad you didn't ask me to open my gift in front of this gathering. I don't know if they'll ever be able to think of you as a hardworking man. They seem to think ice cream and sailboards and Day-Glo colors are kid's stuff."

"How about you, what do you think, Kali?"

"I like you, big kid." She stretched to brush her lips across his chin. "But I know it's considered childish to spend money too impulsively."

He pulled her into his arms. "What about spending it on people you care about?" Quinn smoothed his palms down her back, letting them rest on the curve of her derriere.

"Depends on what you bought me," Kali said with a sigh. "You know Morgan's bound to come in here any minute looking for you. What are you going to say to him?"

"What *can* I say? It isn't my place to tell him how to raise his son. I'll apologize for the extravagance, and ask him to allow Travis to keep the gift."

"Morgan will never agree to it, Quinn."

"And I might suggest he try to be more understanding with his son."

"Oh great. Just try suggesting such a thing. It'll make him furious, but you won't be the one to feel the sting. He'll resent me for the next five years just for bringing you here tonight."

"Five years?" Morgan repeated from the kitchen doorway. "Isn't that a bit of an exaggeration, little sister?"

"Morgan!" Kali picked up a dish towel from the counter. "The way you sneak up on people, I swear you walk on air."

"That's nothing. To hear it told, Quinn Sullivan walks on water."

"You wanted to talk to me?" With an aura of calm, Quinn stepped over to the kitchen table and pulled out two chairs.

"Yeah, I do," Morgan replied with a nod, "but I don't suppose I feel as comfortable in a kitchen as you do. Why don't we step out on the back porch?"

"I'd rather sit down at a table to discuss the matter. It's nice and bright in here and we can relax a bit while we talk, don't you think?" Quinn challenged the older man. "Travis might feel more comfortable."

"I already talked to my son in private."

"Dammit, Morgan," Kali cried out. She balled up the dish towel and threw it at her brother. "Did you have to ruin his birthday?"

"You just wait just a minute, Kali," Morgan roared back, clenching the towel in his fist. "You've been mothering that boy for fourteen years but that's over with. He's almost a man now, and I'm the only one ordering him around. I'm tired of my whole family interfering. Deciding things by committee is no way to raise a kid, and for once he's going to see clear that I'm the boss around here."

"What'd you say to him?" Kali demanded, not bothering to brush the tears from her cheeks.

"I told Travis he'd have to return the wet suit to Quinn. And I told him he won't be taking any of those sailing lessons."

"How could you be so cruel?" Kali shook her head. "How upset is he?"

"He's fine." Morgan stalked to the counter and threw the dish towel into the sink. "I won't have my son telling people I've given him permission to do something when I haven't. I won't have him lying."

"Where is he?" Kali demanded a second time.

"Sulking in the barn." Morgan rubbed his jaw. "His feelings are hurt because I yelled at him."

Kali grabbed a jacket off a hook on the wall and opened the back door. "I'll be in the barn."

"Travis never said anything about you giving him permission," Quinn remained seated at the table, staring across the room at Morgan. "He told me there was friction between the two of you. The whole wet suit thing was my idea."

"Lying's lying, Sullivan. And I won't have it."

"I was just trying to explain the situation. Lying's a bad habit, but I think Travis was being pretty straight with me. In fact we had a talk about the problems he was having with you—"

"I don't need you to act as counselor for my kid. I'm beginning to believe you're capable of undoing a lot of the good in Travis. Get this straight. I don't want him learning to boardsail, and he won't be working in your ice cream factory either."

"Morgan—"

"I'm not through. I want you to return the damn wet suit."

"Look, I can understand your concern. But Travis isn't going to turn into a boardhead overnight because I give him a few lessons. He can use my gear and for him, boardsailing can be something he does now and then during leisure time.''

''Leisure time? You think an orchardist has time to hit the beach every time the wind comes up? Travis has responsibilities here on the farm you wouldn't know anything about.'' Morgan folded his arms across his chest and glared at Quinn.

''But it's good exercise—''

''He'll get plenty of that working in the orchards. He's sixteen already, and there's a lot he has to learn. I want my boy to feel proud of the work I do, and already he sees me as someone who didn't have to work hard to learn his job.'' Morgan jabbed his finger in the air to make his point. ''I know it's not glamorous and I don't wear colorful clothes, but I'm honest and hardworking. It's bad enough you're practically living with my sister. I won't have you destroying what I've got with my kid.''

Morgan stalked out of the room, cursing under his breath. He returned and paused in the kitchen doorway. ''I think you better leave, Sullivan. Don't worry about Kali. She can use my truck to get back to her place. Good night.''

Using the back of the worn jacket sleeve, Kali brushed the annoying tears off her cheeks. She was angry with herself for showing her vulnerability in front of Quinn and Morgan. But her brother had hurt her deeply.

There was truth to his accusation. She had offered Travis love and support, and at times she had offered a shoulder to cry on. Had she overstepped her bounds and interfered with Morgan's role as father? Why should she take responsibility for any rebelliousness Travis showed? Why didn't Morgan credit her for the boy's strong points?

It didn't matter. The scales were uneven when it came to gratitude. Travis needed her strength now, not her tears or her petty thoughts. She broke into a light run toward the old barn, then paused inside the dimly lit entry to listen for any sounds that might help her find her nephew.

"Travis!" she called out in a near reverent whisper. "Where are you? Answer me!"

After ten minutes of fervent searching, cursing and prayer, she climbed the ladder to the loft.

"You're going to break your neck, Kali. Don't you ever think to carry a flashlight? I'm over here by the hay doors." Travis cracked one of the doors and let light from the security lamp stream inside.

Kali found him sitting on a bale of hay next to two of his cats.

"I thought you might appreciate a friend, sport." She dropped down beside him and picked up Sunburn, a pinky-orange longhair with what appeared to be white tan lines.

"Thanks for the photo album of my mom, Kali," Travis murmured. "I've never seen most of those pictures. I bet you went through a lot of work to find them." He continued stroking Slug Bait, his lethargic tabby.

"I enjoyed doing it, Travis. I'm sorry things didn't go all that smoothly for you tonight. Part of that might be my fault. I should have warned Quinn to stay out of the conflict between you and Morgan."

"It's not Quinn's fault. You can't run ahead of me all my life, Kali, warning people to stay clear of my dad. I have to confront him myself. He has to realize I'm not a kid anymore. If I work steady at Queensland Ice, I'll get my own car. He can't stop me from getting wheels—"

"I think you might be feeling angry and hurt and frustrated, and saying things you don't mean. But it helps to talk. What do you want from Morgan right now, Travis?"

"To be treated like an adult."

"But you just turned sixteen. You have a couple years of growing left to do. I mean right now—what could he do to make you forgive him tonight?"

"I don't know. Maybe just to sit down and talk quietly like we used to, you know, when we'd go fishing together?"

"What do you think Morgan needs from you?"

"You mean something other than slave labor?"

"That's not what I mean. Your father has feelings too. Maybe you've been turning Quinn into a sort of hero for yourself and you've hurt your Dad."

"It's not my fault. It's easy to look up to Mr. Sullivan. He's successful and he's traveled and—"

"I know all about Quinn, Travis. You don't have to convince me."

"Do you love him, Kali?"

"What?"

"Do you—"

"I heard you. I just can't believe you're asking me that question."

"You don't know yet?"

"No, and even if I did, I'm cautious. You know me. I like being certain about things."

"I thought love was more automatic than that."

"It is, Travis. I'm just extra careful. I don't like to make mistakes."

"How could it be a mistake to fall in love?"

"It'd be a mistake if you thought it was love and it wasn't."

"So when will you know for sure? How do you tell?"

Kali looked down at Sunburn's upturned face. The cat seemed to be waiting anxiously for the answer.

"How can I say? It seems to get more complicated as time goes by. Tonight for example..." She felt her throat grow tight. "Quinn was anxious to watch you open your presents and—"

"And?"

"I realized how important it was for him to accept you and your father into his life. Quinn seems to get along well in family gatherings and I felt optimistic. Everything sort of fell in place for a minute."

"So you love Quinn."

"I didn't say that. Now that I know about the wet suit I have to wonder if he was just excited about being generous or if he was... now I'm not so sure."

"You're going to be just like Aunt Zepha. You'll sit and wonder things to death. Maybe you should just believe the feeling for a while until you find out for sure."

"Travis, how did we get on the subject of Quinn Sullivan?"

"I think it's a good subject. See, I want to know more about the boardsailing lesson he gave you."

"Hold on, Travis, I didn't come out to the barn to rehash my ten hour lesson."

"Ten hours? Did you really learn to water start?"

"Hey, let me warn you about those water starts..."

Eleven

Kali took a sip from her cup of herbal tea then continued playing solitaire on the kitchen table. She glanced up at the clock and sighed. Blossom was curled in her lap, yawning and stretching occasionally to remind her owner there were better places to sleep, preferably upstairs.

Kali allowed her gaze to rest for a moment on the skimpy piece of iridescent purple fabric on the far end of the table. She'd gotten home from Morgan's house more than three hours earlier and found a gift-wrapped box from Quinn on her doorstep. The daring single-piece swimsuit had provoked a self-conscious laugh. The note accompanying it had produced tears. But then it had been a night for tears.

She recalled the hug Travis had given her before she left Morgan's farm. She would never please her brother. Why did she expect Morgan to accept his son without conditions?

Pushing her thoughts of Travis and Morgan aside, Kali put down the deck of cards in her hand, picked up the slip of paper and reread it.

Dear Kali,
Here's to the next Pro-Am Champion. May the wind be always at your back and may you walk on water forever.

Quinn

Her eyes misted over again. Where was he? With Blossom's help, she'd checked the motor home and walked through a portion of his unfinished house. His Jeep was there but no Quinn. Had Morgan upset him that much?

It was fear more than concern consuming her tonight. Somewhere deep within she'd always feared his wanderlust. Maybe her reluctance to love or admit her love was centered in that fear. Loving and losing.

"Come on, let's get lucky." Picking up the deck of cards, she tried to muster more enthusiasm for her game of solitaire. She had to hunt to find a complete deck of cards. It'd been ages since she even thought of doing anything so self-involved. Her mother would have kept score on a notepad off to the side. But Kali didn't want to think of rules and score keeping tonight. She felt like cheating. More than just a little.

Solitaire had been her family's game. It began with her mother, who often sat up late waiting for Kali's father to come home. Even at an early age, Kali frequently kept her mother company late into the night. They made a habit of playing double solitaire. Each alone in their game but together in spirit, her mother had assured her then. And sometimes her father joined them. When Morgan played, the game became a competition with teams and elaborate rules.

Kali imagined a future with Quinn Sullivan. He'd been absorbed in the construction of the plant and the house this spring and early summer so he hadn't traveled or sought excitement outside of boardsailing on the Columbia. Would all that change when the house and plant were completed?

By his own admission, Quinn was a rootless, free-spirited man. Was she already stepping on his precious freedom robe? Kali wondered if her children would be sitting up late with her. Would double solitaire continue for another generation?

No, she ordered the unformed image from her mind. It wasn't fair to Quinn. He was a half-a-year man, but that didn't make him half a man. There would be a way to work things out. The sooner she gave up the struggle, the sooner she could know whether it was really love that drew her to him. And in loving with her whole heart, would the rest fall in place? Would the answers suddenly be there?

The tea was tepid and the room was growing colder. For the past six weeks Quinn had shared her bed nightly. What would it be like to wake up in the morning without him? What would it be like to feel his absence six months out of the year?

She'd wrestled with these fears and doubts since she'd arrived home. Maybe longer. Perhaps they'd been on her mind since Quinn's return to Hood River.

Tonight, had the intense feelings toward him been her own desire to dismiss these fears and give fully of herself? He could walk through the door any minute. She wanted to be prepared. Instead she was cradling a cat in her lap, holding the ten of diamonds and looking for a jack.

A sudden noise made her start. The deck fell out of her left hand spilling cards across the table. Blossom stood and stretched, then thumped her head against Kali's shoulder. "It's just the wind," Kali reassured the cat and herself.

The wind. It was a constant here in the Columbia River Gorge, an ever-present force that had howled in and out of her life since birth. Never before had she been so aware of its presence.

If she loved Quinn . . . and if she were to lose him, how would the pain have a chance to heal? She would have to leave Hood River and her family and the winds behind to escape his memory.

She lifted Blossom from her lap and looked into the cat's questioning eyes. "Should we go upstairs and call it a night, kitty? Just you and me like the old days?"

"Damn, Sullivan. You look like hell this morning. Mind if I join you for breakfast?" Without waiting for Quinn's consent, Jack, his sailing partner, slid into the booth across from him.

"I ought to sue all those cigarette companies for false advertising," Quinn grumbled good-naturedly as he ran his fingers through his windblown hair. "You know how they romanticize the solitary man in their ads?"

"But you don't smoke."

"Of course not. I just got sort of hung up on that image. There was some trouble with Kali's brother last night, and I was in the middle of it. Spending the night walking the beaches and hitching rides through the gorge seemed like a real macho thing to do. I about froze my butt off out there last night."

"I wondered what you were doin' in here eatin' that big breakfast." Jack opened the menu. "You wanna talk about it?"

"I guess so." Quinn explained the problem in brief. "I keep trying to figure out how I could have handled the situation differently. I know how impressionable kids his age are."

"I think the kid's father has more that one problem to contend with. He doesn't want you seeing his sister. You're an outsider. And his son is probably showing more respect for you than he is for his father. That would bother anyone, I'd think."

"Yeah, evidently Travis talks about me a lot at home."

"Must be bothering you quite a bit if you spent the whole night walking and thinking about it."

"I've caused a falling out between Morgan and Kali. You know I'm building my house right next door to Kali's farm, and she lives next to her brother's. How am I going to live in harmony with my closest neighbors—well, Kali's a hell of a lot more than a neighbor, Jack. But still, I've got to find a way to resolve the problem before there's some kind of permanent rift in her family. I don't want that on my conscience. Family means a lot to her.''

"At least you're thinking about it," Jack became engrossed in eating his breakfast.

Quinn wrapped his hands around the mug of hot coffee in front of him and looked out the window at downtown Hood River. He knew the answers weren't found in one or two conversations with close friends or in a nightlong roadside adventure.

After leaving Morgan's farm, he'd left his Jeep at home and hitched a ride into town with thoughts of an all-night drunk on his mind. By the time he'd reached a bar, he'd realized dulling his feelings was no longer the mature way to deal with them.

He'd hurt Travis, dangling gifts and the promise of lessons before the boy's eyes only to have to take them away. And there was still the matter of the job to settle. A sixteen-year-old had the right to take any job he wanted. Morgan couldn't forbid Quinn from hiring his son. At least that option was open. Perhaps it'd make up for the loss of the wet suit and boardsailing lessons.

Then there was the matter of Kali. Maybe she was right. It was childish to give in to impulses and buy extravagant gifts. It'd hurt him to hear her say it. But dammit, Quinn swore to himself as he sipped his coffee, he had money to spare. That made him different, an exception.

But money wasn't the issue for him right now. Commitment was. When he arrived back at Hood River he was willing to commit himself to starting the

North American plant for Queensland Ice. Committing to a woman was another matter. Perhaps it was linked to his fear of too much security, his association of security with boredom.

Even if he wanted a long-term relationship, did she feel the same way about him?

And what about the partnership agreement he'd signed in Australia?

"Heard the wind conditions yet?" Jack interrupted Quinn's reverie.

"You said I looked like hell when you walked in here. You think I'm taking a board out?" Quinn rubbed the stubble on his chin and chuckled. "I'm catching some sleep then making a decision."

"You make it sound like life or death, Sullivan."

"It is. Some things are a little more important than life or death."

"All right, that's the last of the hand washables," Kali said aloud to herself as she rinsed out a peach-colored bra and patted it dry between towels.

"Let's put you in the laundry basket with your friends and—" she lifted the basket of lingerie and shouldered the screen door open "—we'll all go out to the clothesline to make use of the sunshine, and you guys will get some nice fresh air."

Immediately after awakening, she'd busied herself with a long list of chores. The pain of last night was less intense when her mind and body were totally preoccupied. And when she talked to herself.

Singing along to a tune on her country and western station, she began hanging up the satin-and-lace confections that were her sole obsession.

Thinking that washing lingerie would keep her mind off her troubles had been a mistake. Every time she looked at a delicate undergarment, she recalled memories of Quinn. Was there anything that didn't have a bit of emotional history woven in?

Nothing was working. Talking to herself just made her realize there was no one to answer her. Kali recalled the many times he'd met her in the orchard or in the kitchen after a long day of work, teasing her about the sexy creations she wore beneath her plain T-shirts and jeans.

"It's three o'clock, people," she addressed the lineup of lingerie swaying in the breeze with a laugh. "Mr. Sullivan hasn't called or left a note or dropped by." What could Morgan have said to Quinn that might have upset him like this? She anguished over the question. Anything was possible. And when Morgan dropped by to pick up his truck at noon, he had refused to discuss it.

"Let's complicate the day even more, Kali, by dwelling on whether you should tell Quinn you've given a lot of thought to the question of whether you love him." She reached up to pin an especially memorable satin pajama top to the nylon clothesline. "I think I love you," she said softly holding the arms of the pajama top out. "Would you believe me if I said I love you? Would *I* believe it?"

She'd never said those three words to any man. She'd never considered saying it until now...with Quinn.

"Kali, I'd say you have an X-rated clothesline."

She dropped the arms of the pajama top and whirled to find Quinn standing some distance behind her, leaning against her old birch tree. Had he heard her? Or were her words drowned out by the country and western tune playing on the radio? He seemed distant, his attention moving from her to the lingerie swaying in the wind.

"Were you talking to yourself just now?" he asked as he stepped forward.

"I think everyone does it now and then when they're upset." Kali turned around and picked a lacy nightie out of the laundry basket. The silence that followed was painful, but she concentrated on her task.

"Strange—you're able to talk to yourself but not to me?" Quinn sounded hurt. He moved up behind her and touched her shoulder gently. "About last night—"

"I went to the barn to find Travis, and when I got back Morgan said you'd left in a huff. He told me to take his truck home."

"He asked me to leave the house, Kali. And he wasn't subtle about it."

"Morgan and subtle are like oil and water. I waited up for you last night."

"I needed time alone. Please try to understand, Kali. I was angry at myself for stirring up trouble with your family."

"I knew you would be. I feel so helpless. I can't begin to guess what the solution is." She shook her head. Taking a clothespin out of the pocket of her sundress, she finished hanging up the nightie.

"I think it's obvious that I'm a big part of the problem." Quinn took his hand away from her shoulder and stepped to the other side of the clothesline.

She left her hands on the line for a moment, pulling the nylon cord down slightly so she could see his face. "I want Travis to respect his father, but I feel Morgan has to earn a portion of that respect."

"But he doesn't need competition, Kali. And this matter with your brother and nephew only complicates the issues that stand between us."

"I'm not sure what issues you're talking about, Quinn." Kali loosened her grip on the clothesline slightly. She could still see Quinn's eyes and they told all.

"The issues that made me stay up all night and walk the beaches. I talked to myself quite a bit last night, too, Grasshopper." Lifting the clothesline up, he reached out with his arm and pulled her through, dampening her shoulders on the freshly washed lingerie.

He brushed her hair back from her forehead and touched her cheek. "Kali, I don't know how to tell you this."

"You're leaving, going away, aren't you?"

"How did you know?"

"Just a feeling. You're treating me like fine china. You never do that. And you're carrying the weathered bush hat you wore the day you came back to

Hood River, the day of the parade—'' Her voice broke and she swallowed hard. "I could only guess it would be something painful."

"Painful for both of us. It's just for a couple of weeks, I promise. I can't tell you everything. Some of it involves business contracts and partnership agreements. It's complicated."

"I guess I'm a little surprised. Between the house and the ice cream plant, this is such a busy time for you."

"Albert Ortiz is in charge at the plant. He's more than capable. Besides, we won't be in full production for some time. I've suspended hiring until I return. As for the house, they'll be moving the furniture in by the end of next week. I can always rearrange it later." He gave her a halfhearted smile. She studied the lines of strain around his mouth.

"You can tell me where you're going and maybe why."

"Australia. I'll be in Queensland." He slipped the hat onto his head. "As for why, I need to see if I can rearrange my life so I can spend more time here. And I need to do more thinking...for the sake of the neighborhood."

"You're being cryptic as usual. What neighborhood?"

"Mine. Yours. Ours. Morgan's. If I'm going to live in Hood River, I'm going to have to find a way to come back here and live peacefully with my neighbors."

"Is that what I am now? A neighbor?"

"You know better, Kali. I'm not choosing my words well. Please, don't make this any harder on me than it already is."

"I could say the same thing to you, Quinn."

"I know." He glanced at his watch. "Jack's packing the Jeep. He's going to rush me to Portland to catch the flight. I told you I'll be back in a few weeks. No later." He paused and smiled. "Give me something to dream on. Tell me, how does the swimsuit fit?"

"I look scandalous."

"I bet you shimmer." Quinn took her in his arms and simply held her for what seemed an eternity. The sharing of their warmth was more intimate than any kiss. Kali was struck by the desire to tell Quinn of the intensity of her feelings.

A horn sounded from the front of the farmhouse.

"There's Jack. Impatient, as usual," Quinn explained as he began walking towards the driveway and the noisy Jeep. "There's a phone number at the office with Albert. I can't guarantee I'll be there when you call, but they can reach me in an emergency."

She had never flown anywhere in her life. At the moment, mention of air travel conjured up images of the airport scene from *Casablanca*. Quinn surrounded by a fog that would soon envelop her. Would time stand still until he returned?

"Damn. I keep feeling as though I've forgotten something." Reaching into his pocket, Quinn pulled out his passport. "I've got that, but is there anything else I need?" he seemed to be addressing the question

to her in a distracted sort of way as he searched another pocket.

"Yes, there is," Kali half choked, her throat burning with unshed tears. "Quinn, you need to know how
much I care about you."

He took his hand from his pocket and stared at her,
his expression unreadable.

As seconds slipped by in silence, Kali felt a physical
ache invade her chest. How many times last night had
she wondered if the words "I love you" might over-
power Quinn's wanderlust?

She didn't feel certain about using them to describe
her feelings. She could cheat at solitaire. Real life was
another matter. Their relationship was built on honesty. As helpless and powerless as she felt, she
wouldn't declare her love in an attempt to make him
stay.

"I'll miss you, Quinn," she shook her head, unable to believe he would really leave. "I'll miss all the
warmth you bring to my life."

"Hold the thought, Grasshopper," he whispered as
he bent to give her a warmly ravaging kiss, "and I'll
hold the feeling."

Jack honked again and Quinn pulled away reluc-
tantly and scrambled into the waiting Jeep.

As dust rose in the gravel driveway, Kali stopped
smiling. "Hold the thought," she repeated aloud.
"I'm not going to spend the next week or two pining
away for Quinn Sullivan. I'm going to fill my calendar with dates. Dates with myself!"

Twelve

———

"What's wrong with this picture, Ms. Rainwater?" Heather asked in a lazy drawl.

"There's nothing wrong with two female orchardists working in an orchard."

"Working on their tans? Kali, you're crazy. Why don't we go down to the beach and do this for real?"

"Because I'm going to have tan lines this year if it kills me, but I refuse to appear in public in this swimsuit. *Yet.*"

Kali sighed contentedly, enjoying the warmth of the summer sun. "Tell me, Heather, when was the last time the two of us spent an afternoon sunbathing in an apple orchard, or anywhere else for that matter, and discussing love, exercise and clothing styles?"

"I think we had a day like this back in the summer after the seventh grade."

"Could be."

"But, Kali, we didn't have your wonderful strawberry wine back then."

"We were children."

"Let's toast to lost innocence, to the carefree days of childhood and this year's harvest—"

"Stop! Stop! I didn't bring *that* much wine, Heather."

"It'll be a composite toast. Cheers."

Kali laughed and lifted her glass. "Cheers."

"Nap time," Heather said with a yawn. "Sunshine and wine..."

Kali smiled at her sleeping friend then applied a new layer of suntan oil to her glistening body. Her natural pigment was tan enough by some standards, but that wasn't the point. She wanted tan lines, evidence that she hadn't spent the period of Quinn's absence sadfaced and closeted in the house.

It would have been so easy to give in to the letdown that occurred soon after the dust settled in the driveway and the roar of the Jeep could no longer be heard.

She chose to keep firm to her resolution of making dates with herself. Aside from her routine work, her calendar was full of picnics and outings and reminders to take time for herself. She planned each day as a challenge to her old way of life. And she wanted to discover how full or empty her life might be if she gave serious consideration to loving a half-a-year man like Quinn.

For six months out of the year she might be alone, and if she was going to hold any thought, it had to be the thought of loving herself first. Loving herself enough to enjoy the solitude that had once been her shroud. It had to be her newfound mantle whether she chose to commit to a life with Quinn or not.

Kali sighed and stretched her arms overhead. Her blanket and towel offered little comfort from the bumpy ground. "Lumps," she whispered to no one, allowing herself to be fully aware of the uneven ground beneath her. How could she complain about the lumpy landscape when she was enjoying the serene luxury of sunbathing in her own orchard? This time in the sun was a gift to herself. A gift that would keep on giving because she would feel renewed.

She looked at the trees twenty feet away. A few apples had fallen to the ground, adding their sweet perfume to the earthen smells of the sunbaked field. Despite the dulling effect of the strawberry wine, the sights and smells of this glorious summer day were overwhelming.

Quinn had brought new insight into her life, an awakening that had added beauty to the elements of life she'd begun to take for granted.

Why had it taken a man to open her eyes to this gift that lay within? she pondered. And if knowing Quinn brought the awareness, could it be that losing Quinn might take the gift away?

She blamed her sudden melancholy mood on the wine and told herself when the wine wore off, she'd be back in good spirits for whatever adventure tomorrow would bring. She couldn't possibly be missing Quinn this much.

His absence was felt in the coolness of things. In the middle of the night, she awoke, aware of the cool hollow near her back where his body had warmed her. Her cups of coffee cooled without the topping off ceremony that had become a playful habit at the meals they shared. When the sun set on Rainwater Ridge, Kali was more aware of the chilling winds that buffeted her face and brought tears to her eyes. Quinn had done more than shield her from the cold. He had brought light and warmth to the barren landscape from which her dreams were born. New dreams emerged, powerful, unlimited, born of her new strength.

And yet she remained unsure of her love for Quinn. When he returned, if she could honestly judge herself a stronger person for having spent the time without him, she would have a better sense of whether life with Quinn was a realistic choice for her.

"This is crazy, Kali," Morgan grumbled as Kali and Travis climbed into the large rowboat. "You must have a bee in your bonnet if you think the three of us can sit in that thing for more than twenty minutes without having a man, woman or full-grown child overboard."

"Try to cooperate, Morgan. Here, hand me the bag of sandwiches." Kali groaned as she reached for the sack. "I wanted to do something with the two of you this week. A family outing."

"That's choice. We're usually on the outs," Travis commented from the back of the rowboat.

"Cheer up you two. Good Lord, Morgan, why is this bag so heavy?" She stood to get a better grip on their picnic lunch.

"I brought a few beers. We haven't gotten two feet from shore and already she's standing up in the boat. The captain says sit down. I'm casting off." After untying the line, Morgan pushed the boat off shore and climbed in. "I'll row," he announced moving to the center.

What makes you the captain? Kali bit her tongue and chose instead to burn a hole in Morgan's back with her scowl. She was determined to make the boat ride and picnic enjoyable for her nephew's sake. For *her* sake, she made a mental correction.

In the days since the disastrous birthday party, Travis had been too busy to miss Quinn Sullivan. Morgan had added to the boy's chores, dimming any hopes of a summer job outside of the farm.

"So now," Morgan caught his breath, "what are we supposed to do while I row my boat around my lake until it's time to eat?"

"We can talk and get some sun and you know..." Kali paused. "Just being near the water relaxes most people. We can appreciate the fact that we have each other."

"Kaaali, pleeassse." Travis made retching motions from the front of the boat. "Why are you being so noticeably cheerful all the time? I hope you're not just trying to make me feel better."

"I'm working on a sort of self-improvement program, Travis."

"Amazing how this burst of social visits and self-improvement coincides with Quinn Sullivan's exit to Australia," her brother remarked. Morgan's tone had changed to one of interest. "You're not planning to idle away all the hours until his return, are you?"

"I'm learning to enjoy time by myself," she countered. "I'm doing things I should have been doing all these years. You might benefit from my example."

"You call this *time by yourself*? Why did you bring us along?" Morgan paused to take off his shirt.

"Because being with Quinn has taught me the value of family ties."

"Oh yeah? How's that?" Morgan picked up the oars again and resumed rowing.

"His are shot, Dad," Travis offered.

"His what?"

"Quinn's family ties."

"I should have figured," Morgan chuckled. "He's too busy getting involved with other people's families to work out his own problems."

"A little to your left, Captain," Kali spoke through cupped hands. "You're steering us into the reeds off starboard bow."

"I knew that. I'm giving you a tour of the vast wildlife refuge we operate here on beautiful Lake Rainwater."

"That's why we—" Travis bowed his head "—the overworked caretakers of this private lake, let the reeds get out of hand. It makes boating a lot safer."

"It's hard not to avoid them," Morgan strained against the oars. "And that's not starboard, Kali. It's port."

"It doesn't matter what it is, Dad," Travis motioned with both arms. "Turn! Turn!"

All three of them laughed at the sound of reeds scraping the sides and bottom of the boat.

"I wonder how deep it is these days out there toward the center." Kali pointed. "Looks like a good place to picnic, and maybe we can measure the depth too."

Fifteen minutes later, Kali was smiling as she reached for the sack of sandwiches. It was a rare opportunity for her to see Morgan and Travis cajoling with one another, even about sensitive subjects such as chores and summer jobs. It seemed the humor set up a defense that let them approach one another without getting too close to real feelings. And it was obvious Travis was limiting his mentions of Quinn Sullivan.

She was elated that her attempt at a family outing was a success. The tuna fish sandwiches were devoured while Morgan and Kali reminisced about childhood summers.

"Let's get some idea of how deep the center is," Morgan suggested as he moved to the front of the boat and picked up the bleach-bottle-filled-with-cement anchor. "I think the rope is marked by feet if I remember. It's been a long time—oops!"

Morgan dropped the anchor through the bottom of the old boat. The thud was followed by the crunch of old wood and the whoosh of water running into the bow.

"Did we bring life jackets?" Kali shouted as she tried to stop the flow with clothing and their paper lunch sack. "Of course not," she answered herself. "But forget I mentioned it and stay calm anyway."

"Yeah," Morgan laughed nervously, gripping an oar. "Especially important since...we have no idea how deep it is. Boy, do I feel stupid."

"It's all right, Dad. Move back." Travis reached out for his father's hand. "You might get your foot stuck in the hole and go down with the boat."

"Like a real captain. Lord, is this humbling." Using the oar, Morgan rearranged the water-soaked clothing in the bow. He looked at Kali with frightened eyes. "It's going down. Let's swim to shore. Everyone set?"

"But we just ate," Kali felt giggles coming on as she prepared to abandon ship. "We gotta wait an hour."

"Don't worry, it was tuna-fish!" Travis shouted just before he hit the water.

Kali and Morgan waited for the rowboat to sink knee deep then stepped out and began swimming behind Travis.

"I was just thinking something," Morgan sputtered. "Either the reeds will save us or it'll be cut-grass and we'll get shredded to ribbons before we make shore."

"There's no such thing as cut-grass," Kali scoffed. She kept a watchful eye on her brother who'd never been a strong swimmer.

"Let's slow down a bit, Travis!" She was relieved when they swam three abreast at a slower pace.

After traversing through the reeds, Kali followed the others onto the grassy bank and lay on her back in a sodden heap.

Morgan was the first to sit up. "*'Just being near the water relaxes most people.'*" He did a near perfect imitation of her earlier statement. She joined their uproarious laughter until her sides hurt.

"The boat wouldn't have sunk so fast, Dad, if you hadn't brought that case of beer along."

"It was only half a six-pack of *light* beer. I thought Kali might want one."

Travis sat up and gave his father a friendly poke in the arm. "And you probably want me to swim back out there and salvage what's left, right?"

"Wrong." Morgan shook his head. His smile softened. "You work hard enough as it is, son. On top of that, think of all the energy you expend just aggravating me." He ran his hands through his dripping black hair, leaving it spiked with grooves. "It's like a fulltime job for you."

"Naw, it's more of a hobby," Travis played along.

"Oh yeah? Some hobby." Morgan grumbled. "I found a gray hair yesterday and it's got your name on it, Travis."

Her nephew laughed as he pulled his wet shirt over his head. Kali watched as the smiling teenager combed his fingers through the shock of hair at his forehead and pushed it back. The banter continued. Father and son were sitting side by side on the grass, their waterslickened bare chests and shoulders glistening in the sunlight, their dark hair combed into furrows, their tanned faces creased with laughter.

The Rainwater's Chinook ancestry had been diluted, but Kali recognized the strong family traits that had persevered generation after generation. The black hair and intense deep-set eyes, high cheekbones and the full lower lip. And the pride. She recalled her father's proud profile, authoritative stance and the thunder in his voice.

The torch had been passed to Morgan in a sense, and there was pain in this kind of parenting. Working closely with your children while they struggled through the rebellious teenage years had to dampen the joy of seeing them pick up the skills needed for taking over a farm.

Was pride a dominant gene? She'd inherited the same dark features. Was her pride so strong that it was interfering with her ability to declare her feelings for Quinn?

She thought about the future family outings she'd planned. How would Morgan and Travis feel if her plans included Quinn Sullivan? How would he have fit into today's adventure? Kali stared at the shimmering lake and wondered. Would he have concentrated on rescuing her and never allowed her a chance to find her strength? Would Quinn have ridiculed Morgan in any way for dropping the anchor and sinking the boat?

No. She knew the answers. Quinn was fair and honest. And no matter what lay ahead in their future, she intended to avoid becoming overly dependent on him as a helpmate, a neighbor...or a lover. She would learn to return to her old ways of doing for herself.

"Thanks, Aunt Kali," Travis said. "I know I was giving you a bad time before, but I'm glad you thought this thing up. It was fun. What's next on our list of family outings?"

"White-water rafting," Kali announced.

"Let's throw her back in the lake, son."

Thirteen

Biting her lip, Kali tore open the manila envelope and quickly scanned the letter. "We've done it, Grandma!" she cried aloud. She scooped the large white cat from the porch railing and showed her feline companion the letter. "My patent's been approved, Blossom!" The cat showed little interest in anything other than the ribbon trailing from the braid that hung over Kali's shoulder.

Kali set the cat down, took a deep breath and walked absently to the side porch that wrapped around the house. She leaned over the railing. Finally there was validation, proof that her work had produced results. She'd receive royalties for the propagation of Grandma Rainwater's extra-sweet berry.

Fragments of past and present dreams filled her thoughts. She sat back in the porch swing and rocked, unable to resist hugging herself and smiling. She was enjoying a momentary escape from the hot August sun and basking in the glory of her accomplishment.

So many dreams had been hatched here on the old swing. She lay down full-length on the wooden slats and gathered momentum with an occasional push of her hand.

"If only Quinn were here," she found herself thinking. Despite her two weeks of making time for herself and filling every spare hour, she missed him dearly. This special moment would be more complete if he were here to share her news.

Kali turned her head and stared at the scene beyond. Quinn's house had been completed as scheduled. The furniture had been moved in while she accompanied Morgan and Travis on a one-day white-water rafting trip. She fingered the manila envelope absently. She held one dream in her hand, but it paled slightly when she thought of past dreams, dreams that included a house on Rainwater Ridge.

She swallowed hard. If she had told Quinn she loved him when they said goodbye beside the Jeep, would he have concluded his business in Australia quickly and arrived back home sooner than planned?

The questions were endless and served no purpose. Words and fancy phrasing didn't come easy for her. She preferred honesty and concise language. But the subject of love seemed to need something softer. She shivered as she thought of Quinn's return.

"Kali! Kali!" A recognizable male voice called from the front of the house.

"Morgan, I'm on the side porch." Kali felt an uneasy tingling sensation as she sat up. "What's wrong, what is it?'' she asked as her brother rounded the corner of the house.

"I tried calling you.'' Morgan's agitation was evident. "It's Travis!''

"Is he hurt?'' Kali was on her feet in seconds.

"He's not hurt! At least I don't think so.''

"Where is he?''

"That's why I'm here! We had an argument last night, you know how we're getting busy with the pear harvest, and he wanted to take off with some of his friends. He must have left this morning...''

"Calm down, Morgan.'' Kali felt a wave of relief. "It doesn't sound that serious. How far can he get on his bike?''

"Bike? Kali, he's got my pickup. Ever since he got his driver's license last week, he's been testing me.''

"Damn. I thought you two were working things out. Did you look for a note?'' Kali picked up the rest of her mail from the porch railing and quickly shuffled through it. "Nothing here. There must be some indicator of where he's going.''

"There is,'' Morgan folded his arms across his chest. "I called his friends. They were all at home, which means he's alone and...according to one of them, he planned to do some boardsailing.''

"Well, he doesn't have any gear. We just have to check the rental places down near the Marina and we'll—''

"He didn't rent anything, little sister.'' Morgan's fists were clenched and his jaw rigid. "I called the rental shops—every one of them. Then I stopped at Quinn Sullivan's place and sure enough, someone's broken into his storage shed where his gear is kept.''

"No." Kali dropped her mail into a wicker chair. "Travis wouldn't take Quinn's gear without—"

The sound of the Jeep's engine interrupted their conversation. Quinn parked in Kali's driveway and in a fluid graceful movement, vaulted out of the vehicle.

"Kali!" His shout brought her out of her momentary fog, and she was down the stairs and into his arms in seconds. "Lord, have we got a lot to talk about!" He laughed as he wrapped her in a warm embrace and lifted her off the ground. "Look at you, so tanned and even more beautiful than I remember!"

"Quinn, it's Travis. He's missing!" Kali looked from Quinn's stricken expression to her brother.

"I'm pretty sure he broke into your storage area last night or this morning, Sullivan." Morgan quickly filled in the details.

"I'll run up to the house and check my gear to see what's missing." Quinn released his hold on Kali. "Then I'll call up Jack and see if he can help us search the local spots and drive through the parking lots. I should get a wind report, too."

"Come on, Morgan," Kali took her brother's arm. "Why don't we go inside and make some coffee and sandwiches. You can call Mom in Portland to see if Travis had long-distance plans."

"How's it look?" she asked Quinn twenty minutes later when he walked into her kitchen.

"Strong winds. I'm worried. And it's not just because Travis is inexperienced. If he's still angry, he won't be aware of the dangers."

"Sullivan, I'm sorry about him breaking into your gear like that." Morgan handed Quinn a cup of coffee. "I'll pay any expenses, of course."

"Don't worry about it. Right now, I'm more concerned about finding Travis." Quinn swallowed a few mouthfuls. "Kali, there's a chance he's headed for one of the inland lakes, knowing we'd be looking for him around here. Do you want to start calling the resorts and asking if he's been spotted? A lot of them sell food and bait, and chances are he got hungry."

"Good idea," Kali nodded her agreement, picked up the phone book and began making a list.

"Did he take one of those wet suits of yours?" Morgan asked, his face etched with concern. "I was thinking about how cold the water can get."

"I never returned the wet suit I bought for his birthday," Quinn admitted with some reluctance. "It's the only one missing from storage—"

"I'm just glad to hear he had the sense to think about hypothermia."

"It's early August, Morgan." Kali gave her brother a light hug. "Don't worry. He'll be all right. I wonder who suffers more, the parents or the kid with growing pains."

"Kali, we'll split up and check back with you from time to time to see if he shows up." Kali watched as Quinn jotted a number down and handed it to her brother. "Morgan, take this. We're neighbors. I think it's time you had my phone number."

Two hours later, Kali felt she had imposed on every resort owner in the entire area. Quinn, Morgan and Jack had all called the house regularly. There was still no sign of Travis.

"Lewis Lake?" she was asking when Morgan and Quinn walked through the front door. "How long ago? Can you see the truck from the store? Uh-huh. Right, boardsailing gear. What's he wearing? Good. No, that's good news. We're on our way. Thank you for calling back!"

"He's at Lewis Lake!" she announced. "Travis just got there. He bought a bag full of munchies and hasn't changed into the wet suit yet. We can all fit into my truck."

"It'll take about an hour to get there." Morgan was already half way out the door.

"I'm going to load more gear." Quinn held up his hand. "Just in case."

"Just in case what?" she asked, perplexed.

"In case I need to get out on the water. I had a chance to teach you self-rescue. Travis has probably never heard of it. Let's hope he doesn't have to learn it the hard way."

An hour later, Kali found herself sandwiched between Quinn and Morgan, and having serious doubts about the future of her extended family.

The first half of the journey had consisted of Quinn attempting to shed light on Travis's actions by describing his own youthful misadventures and the problems he encountered with his autocratic father. Morgan debated every point bluntly.

The second half of the journey consisted of a tension-filled conversation on the subject of revoking driving privileges.

"I'm going to take his driver's license away until school starts," Morgan reiterated for the fourth time.

When he wasn't debating about driving privileges, her brother was questioning his own parenting skills.

"Don't be so hard on yourself," she attempted to comfort Morgan. "Last week, Travis told me he'd been upset that my relationship with Quinn had limited the time I could spend with him. I feel guilty too, but I know that isn't going to help anyone."

"I started having a relationship with a woman last year," Morgan announced out of the blue, keeping his eyes on the gravel road ahead. "I have to think that's when some of the trouble started between Travis and me."

"But you have a right to a full life, Morgan."

"Tell that to my son, Kali."

"I will—right after we rescue him."

The tension eased when Quinn spotted the one-mile marker for Lewis Lake.

"That's him. He's out there toward the center of the lake!" Kali shouted soon after they pulled into the parking lot. "Doesn't he look unsteady, Quinn?"

"Not bad," Quinn said with a trace of pride. "He's doing rather well. I'm suiting up and taking my rig out. You trust me, don't you Morgan?"

"I can't walk on water," Morgan Rainwater said through clenched teeth. "Do I have a choice?"

Quinn had a little trouble catching a wind that propelled him toward Travis. He was agonizing over the situation. Morgan would be furious if he saw him giving his son a boardsailing lesson.

Quinn had to make a choice. It was an opportunity to make a positive imprint on a young mind, to encourage Travis to allow his spirit to soar.

Who was he more obligated to—father or son? Disobey one and disappoint the other? He didn't want to discourage a young man's search for independence and understanding. But he wanted Travis to be realistic about the stress he'd caused others.

The boy was too involved to notice Quinn crossing the lake and approaching.

"Pull it over, buddy!" Quinn teased.

"Quinn!" Travis jerked around and splashed into the water.

"Do you realize it isn't polite to break into other people's storage sheds?"

"I'm sorry. Really sorry." Travis struggled to grab hold of the board. "I just wanted to give this a try. Who else is here?"

"Kali and your father. They're watching from the south shore."

"Oh man, I'm a dead duck."

"I wouldn't say that. You're not doing bad at all. I thought I might give you a few pointers if you have any strength left."

"Not a lot, but this might be my last chance to get a real lesson."

"Then let's start. It looks like you're as stubborn as your aunt when it comes to doing a perfect water start. Let me help you, Travis."

"He's been giving him some kind of lesson for half an hour, Kali." Morgan paced anxiously on the shore. "I thought he was simply going to rescue Travis."

"Maybe the rescue involves getting this compulsion out of your son's system."

"But it's addictive. I've heard people say that. Can you promise me Travis won't get hooked on this sport and want to travel around the world like Quinn?"

Kali noticed Morgan growing strangely silent when Quinn and Travis approached the shore.

"Morgan, you can relax. There was no damage to any of the equipment," Quinn assured him before he began unzipping his wet suit. "I hope you'll be reasonable about this."

"What do you consider reasonable? My son took my truck without permission, broke into your shed and borrowed what must be a few thousand dollars worth of gear from you, and had us worried for hours. On top of that, he got himself a free boardsailing lesson as a reward."

"That was my idea," Quinn confessed.

Morgan's stern ungiving expression softened. "I'll keep that in mind when I talk to Travis in private."

Kali turned to Quinn. "I think we better start loading the equipment."

"I'll be driving back alone," Morgan announced.

"Alone?" She stared at her brother. "What about Travis?"

"I'd like the two of you to take him for the rest of the day. I need to sort some things out before he comes back home."

"Dad!" Travis called out as Morgan opened the door of the pickup.

"I'll talk to you later, son."

"Look. I'm really sorry, Dad. I don't have any excuses. I really messed up this time and I did it to hurt you, I guess. The way you've hurt me lately. I'm not sure. I just know I didn't accomplish anything."

"I still think it's best you stay with Kali until tonight. Once we get in the truck, I might lose my temper and say the wrong thing, son."

"Dad, wait! I have a suggestion. What if we rent a canoe and do some fishing, maybe buy a picnic lunch and get a chance to talk some things out like we used to?"

"We've got pears to harvest." Morgan began to climb into the pickup.

Kali saw hope for a reconciliation turning into an impasse. Her heart ached for her brother, who only wanted to be the best parent possible. And for Travis, who recognized the foolishness of his actions and desperately wanted to make amends. She struggled for a solution that would appease both.

"Morgan, why don't you take the time to go fishing? I can go over to your place and help out this afternoon," Kali offered.

"And I'll go with her," Quinn stated emphatically.

"But you just flew in from Australia, Sullivan. What about jet lag?"

"I feel great." Quinn put an arm around Kali's shoulder. "Of course, I'll expect a peck of pears for pay."

"I'll *give* you a peck of pears just for saying that!" Morgan responded with a chuckle. "Well, what do you think, Travis? Can you trust me not to drop the anchor in the boat this time?"

"Let me handle the anchor for once, all right?" Travis smiled sheepishly and unzipped the wet suit.

"I have a better idea." Morgan handed a towel to his son. "We'll rent a canoe."

"Thank you," Kali whispered to Quinn as they began putting the gear in her pickup.

"For what?"

"For being the person you are, and for remembering what it's like to be sixteen."

He drew her into an embrace.

"What's wrong, Kali?"

"You're getting me wet."

"Small sacrifice, isn't it?"

"Yes. Very small."

"I have another request, Ms. Rainwater."

"Hmm?"

"Dinner tonight?"

"After all this excitement? We still have to help with the pears and Lord knows what else."

"We'll have good appetites." He kissed her softly. "And we'll need at least eight courses. I have a lot to tell you, and we have a lot to talk about, Grasshopper."

"Why do all the waiters seem to know you?" Quinn asked when their salads were served.

"I had dinner here last week," Kali's exuberant voice almost rose above the polite dinner conversation of the fine Italian restaurant.

Never had he seen her so radiant and strong. The sheen of her long hair, pulled back into a French braid, caught the candlelight and held the glow. She'd added a touch of makeup to her large brown eyes. The sweep of lashes added to their intensity. And her mouth, as always, was soft and welcoming.

"Dinner by yourself? I didn't know you did that sort of thing, Kali."

"After you left, I felt challenged to do a lot of things for the first time and some of them I did just for myself." Her smile faltered for a moment. "But I missed you, Quinn."

"And I missed you." The words were so inadequate. The day had turned to chaos soon after his return that morning. He hadn't had time to express the anguish and indecision he'd gone through for the past two weeks. "You look wonderful."

"Thank you. Your tan looks terrific. Are we going to sit here all night and be polite and compliment each other? I'm dying to find out what happened in Australia."

"I'd rather hear about everything that's happened to you, Kali." What had she done to herself? He knew makeup and lighting could transform a person, but Kali's transformation appeared to be coming from within.

She was wearing a simple black dress with pearls, yet the effect was mesmerizing.

"You said you needed eight courses to get everything in. We're already up to the salad. You start, Quinn. What's on your mind?" Reaching across the table, she took his hand.

"Mostly you, then there's my future and my past. They're all wrapped up together, and I had to spend some time undoing the knots. I've always moved on with my life. I didn't want it cluttered with too much sentimentality. You know I feel too much security might be boring."

"I remember," she said with a laugh.

"Living here in Hood River and watching Travis go through the struggles with Morgan brought up a lot of old memories." Quinn set his salad fork down. "I stopped in California to see my parents and my sister. To say it was emotional would be an understatement. The old hurts have left scars, but we worked around them. My father still prefers to talk money and profits, and he's as conservative as ever."

Quinn reached into his jacket pocket and pulled out a few Polaroids. "I don't want to bore you with photographs, but that's Dad."

Kali studied the picture. "You must look like your mother."

"Thanks, I do. Dad's let himself go. He hasn't played a single sport since high school. We don't have any mutual interests, so finding a common ground for our relationship will always be tough."

Quinn took the photographs back and flipped through them. "He wants to be right all the time, to have the last word."

Quinn began to put the photos away, then paused and left them on the edge of the table, his forefinger touching the white border. "Dad doesn't mean to alienate me, Kali. He just can't help pushing his ideas on me. He always did—and he says he did it because he loved me and wanted me to avoid the pain of making the same mistakes he did."

Quinn looked up, surprised to see tears shimmering in Kali's eyes. "What is it?"

"It touches me that you've given this so much thought. You're trying to work things out. I know it's important to you."

"It's something I've watched you go through for the past five months, since March. You took risks. You've grappled with your problems of family and finances, Kali. I envied your growth, but that didn't help me. I had to see my dad, and I'll have to continue to work on family relationships."

Their entrées were served. Kali looked down at her scampi. When she'd dined alone, she'd been able to taste her food. Tonight, her senses were focused on Quinn.

"You said you were dealing with your future?" she asked in a subtle tone.

"I've worked out a new agreement with my partner in Queensland. I'd be traveling down under only once a year. Even then, it'll be a short stay.

"That's incredible. You'll be here through harvest and Christmas and—"

"Valentine's Day. I felt I needed to sacrifice part of the partnership agreement if I were to be fully committed—to you, love."

Kali touched a finger to the stem of her wine glass. "Fully committed? Quinn, I'm not sure if I understand."

"I love you, Grasshopper." He smiled tenderly and, taking her hand, kissed her fingertips."

"Oh, Quinn." Kali wove her fingers through his. "I've always wanted to be so certain about everything. Since you left I've agonized over the question of loving you. Then yesterday I was in one of my orchards and something came to me. When is an apple really an apple? When it buds or when the blossoms appear or when the fruit appears? Can you really call it an apple before it's ripe?''

"And what conclusion did you reach?"

"That I've loved you from the beginning, even when the feelings between us were budding, and later when they were blooming into something deeper and more lasting.''

"And now?"

"I love you, Quinn."

"I believe you, because I've seen your love reflected in everything you do. But I have to wonder if love is enough. We have a lot to work out—before harvest time.''

"Don't you think that happens in all relationships?''

"Ours is special." He kept her hand locked in his. "It belongs only to us. We have to take good care of it.''

"What's on your mind? Maybe we should begin working on issues now.''

"Okay, for starters I'm worried about your old resentments toward wind smurfs. I just don't see a time when the boardsailors will pack up and leave Hood River, Kali. Knowing how you resent the changes occurring as a result of the influx, I don't know how you can avoid resenting me. The majority of my staff at Queensland Ice will be taken from these people.''

"Maybe we can both learn to live with certain resentments. And gradually work through them. I worried about your wanderlust when you left, wondering if every crisis would mean watching you pack a suitcase. I think we survived the crisis, but it unnerved me. So I decided to use our time apart as an opportunity for me to see if I've become overly dependent on you."

"And your verdict?"

"I like spending time alone. It's not always my first choice, but I look at things from my own perspective. I hold my own opinions."

"And?"

"And I'm not perfect. I realize I have this romanticized view of my hometown as being a place where life is basically simple."

"No one's life is simple."

"I said my view was distorted, romanticized if you like. But give me a little more credit. I've always known the arrival of the boardheads would change my town, but now I realize I'm going through changes too. I think you've helped me see things differently."

"How's that, Kali?"

"I feel it's all right to make mistakes. I want to take more time for myself, to keep my old friendships alive and create new friendships. And I feel there are times when I simply have to trust more."

"And you trust me, love?"

"I trust your intent. I know you can be impulsive. And I feel that led to a lot of the trouble between Morgan and Travis. But this morning when you rescued Travis and showed so much effort in trying to extend the hand of friendship to Morgan, well it meant a lot to me. You were really trying."

"They're a normal father and son, Kali. They'll always have ups and downs."

"They're more than that to me, Quinn. We're an extended family. I helped raise Travis from the time I was fifteen. I think what I'm trying to say is this. When it comes to commitment, my biggest concern is how you'll fit in. *Whether* you'll fit in at all."

"I didn't realize you felt this way, Kali."

"I had a long talk with Travis aboard the stern-wheeler. He told me I hardly had time for him since you came into my life. I feel bad about that. With Dad gone, and Mom living in Portland, I feel I need to maintain that relationship."

"And how do I fit in?"

"I think it's important that you give Morgan's viewpoint more consideration in the future, rather than siding too quickly with Travis. My nephew will probably work with his father most of his life. Respect is important. They'll have to become partners."

"Kali, I feel it's important that Morgan respect his son as well. Travis deserves to be listened to, to be heard out."

"I know. Morgan doesn't always see it that way. And Travis is his son. If you and I are going to continue having a relationship, Quinn, I have to insist that we work on this."

"It's worth working on. Can I bring up an issue of sorts?"

"Certainly. I didn't mean to preach."

"Queensland Ice is still interested in having exclusive use of your strawberry for our ice cream. Would you give it some thought?"

"I forgot to tell you—the patent approval arrived in the mail this morning. I haven't had time to think of the implications. Exclusivity. Hmmm."

"We'd name the flavor Rainwater Red after the berry, and because the berry originated here in Hood River, it will help the public remember the location of our plant . . . and your berry."

"Smart. I'll give it a lot of thought. Tell me, will I be the first in line for a taste test?"

"For the rest of your life, Grasshopper." He paused as he placed her hands between his palms protectively. "That's the level of commitment I'm talking about. I love you. I want to marry you."

"Is this a proposal?" she rasped. Her throat burned, and the ache in her chest eased into a warmth that spread through her body.

"Yes, it's a proposal." He smiled broadly and leaned closer. "I won't be a half-a-year man anymore. I promise I'll be here for you all year, Kali. Every day. We'll be together."

"Together," she whispered. "I like the sound of that word. And I love the thought of forever."

"Is that a yes, Kali?"

"It's a yes and a promise, Quinn."

Reaching up, he touched her cheek. "Why don't we go somewhere more private to celebrate. My house is complete. The furniture was moved in while I was gone. It looks like a real home now. I was hoping you'd be there with me tonight to share it. Sort of a homecoming and housewarming, my love."

Kali took a moment to reflect. Since childhood, she'd thought "dream house" every time she visited

Rainwater Ridge and saw the panoramic view. Perhaps it was a dream shared rather than divided.

"I love you. Take me home, Quinn. To the ridge. Forever."

*   *   *   *   *

 **Silhouette Desire** ®

COMING
NEXT MONTH

#517 BEGINNER'S LUCK—Dixie Browning
Meet September's *Man of the Month*, Clement Barto. Mating habits: unexplored. Women scared him speechless—literally. But with a little beginner's luck, Clem was about to discover something called love....

#518 THE IDEAL MAN—Naomi Horton
Corporate headhunter Dani Ross had to find the right man for a client—but the job title was "Husband." When she met rancher Jake Montana she knew he was ideal—for her!

#519 ADAM'S WAY—Cathie Linz
Business efficiency expert Julia Trent insisted on a purely professional relationship with problem-solver Adam MacKenzie. But he was determined to make her see things Adam's way.

#520 ONCE IN LOVE WITH JESSIE—Sally Goldenbaum
Who says opposites don't attract? Confirmed bachelor Matt Ridgefield had been content with his solitary life-style before carefree, spirited Jessie Sager had come along. The professor had a lot to learn!

#521 ONE TOUCH OF MOONDUST—Sherryl Woods
Paul Reed was the most *romantic* man Gabrielle Clayton had ever met. He was also her new roommate—and suddenly practical Gaby was dreaming of moonlight and magic.

#522 A LIVING LEGEND—Nancy Martin
Hot on the trail of the scoop of the century, Catty Sinclair found only gruff recluse Seth Bernstein. What *was* this gorgeous man doing in the middle of nowhere...?

AVAILABLE NOW:

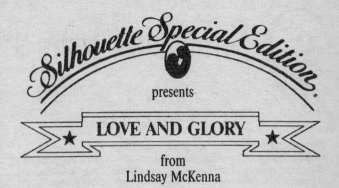

Silhouette Special Edition

presents

★ LOVE AND GLORY ★

from
Lindsay McKenna

Introducing a gripping new series celebrating our men—and women—in uniform. Meet the Trayherns, a military family as proud and colorful as the American flag, a family fighting the shadow of dishonor, a family determined to triumph—with **LOVE AND GLORY!**

June: **A QUESTION OF HONOR** (SE #529) leads the fast-paced excitement. When Coast Guard officer Noah Trayhern offers Kit Anderson a safe house, he unwittingly endangers his own guarded emotions.

July: **NO SURRENDER** (SE #535) Navy pilot Alyssa Trayhern's assignment with arrogant jet jockey Clay Cantrell threatens her career—and her heart—with a crash landing!

August: **RETURN OF A HERO** (SE #541) Strike up the band to welcome home a man whose top-secret reappearance will make headline news . . . with a delicate, daring woman by his side.

Silhouette Intimate Moments®

COMING IN OCTOBER!
A FRESH LOOK FOR
Silhouette Intimate Moments!

Silhouette Intimate Moments has always brought you the perfect combination of love and excitement, and now they're about to get a new cover design that's just as exciting as the stories inside.

Over the years we've brought you stories that combined romance with something a little bit different, like adventure or suspense. We've brought you longtime favorite authors like Nora Roberts and Linda Howard. We've brought you exciting new talents like Patricia Gardner Evans and Marilyn Pappano. Now let us bring you a new cover design guaranteed to catch your eye just as our heroes and heroines catch your heart.

Look for it in October—
Only from Silhouette Intimate Moments!

IMNC-1

Silhouette Intimate Moments®

AWARD OF EXCELLENCE

NORA ROBERTS
brings you the first
Award of Excellence title
Gabriel's Angel
coming in August from
Silhouette Intimate Moments

They were on a collision course with love....

*Laura Malone was alone, scared—and pregnant. She was running
for the sake of her child. Gabriel Bradley had his own problems.
He had neither the need nor the inclination to get involved in
someone else's.*

*But Laura was like no other woman . . . and she needed him. Soon
Gabe was willing to risk all for the heaven of her arms.*

The Award of Excellence is given to one specially selected title per
month. Look for the second Award of Excellence title, coming out in
September from Silhouette Romance—**SUTTON'S WAY**
by **Diana Palmer**

Im 300-1